OUT OF ORDER

To Leo, who shares my dark humour

Susan Knight

Out of Order

Out of Order

is published in 2015 by
ARLEN HOUSE
42 Grange Abbey Road
Baldoyle
Dublin 13
Ireland
Phone/Fax: 353 86 8207617
Email: arlenhouse@gmail.com
arlenhouse.blogspot.com

Distributed internationally by
SYRACUSE UNIVERSITY PRESS
621 Skytop Road, Suite 110
Syracuse, NY 13244–5290
Phone: 315–443–5534/Fax: 315–443–5545
Email: supress@syr.edu

978–1–85132–113–1, paperback

Typesetting by Arlen House

Cover images by Maev Lenaghan

CONTENTS

Out of Order

Horror Show

It's a big grey train, built for the wide gauge of Russian railways.

'Horror show', says the pretty girl in the red dress, shaking her mop of brown curls.

'Is it really?' I ask.

She raises plucked eyebrows in a query. 'A horror show?' She laughs then, bubbles in champagne. 'No, no. *Khorosho*. Is Russian for good'.

'Ah. Yes of course. *A Clockwork Orange*. Good'.

'Clockwork Orange?' She pulls a face.

'Dystopian novel that anglicises Russian words, turns them into gang slang ...'

She laughs again, her teeth glistening, but I can see she doesn't have a clue what I'm talking about. Her name is Irina and she is to be my guide. She speaks English well but with that slippery accent they have. I ask about the rest of the group, a question which confuses her.

'No, you are my only one, David'.

'Suits me', I say. 'Horror show'.

'So, we mount?'

We get on the train. The seats are of slatted wood and don't look comfortable. However, the journey is a short one, according to the brochure. I look at it now. 'Experience of lifetime. Revisit old Soviet Union. Live like Russian peoples in old time communist state'.

You see, I'm not your regular tourist. I like to mix with the locals, go how they go on public transport rather than by taxi, eat where they eat, sleep where they sleep. Oh, I've done the other stuff too, the big museums, the palaces, the luxury shopping, the five star hotels, even the lying on sundrenched beaches oiled all over. Bored to death. So when I picked up the leaflet in my Moscow hotel about a newly opened Soviet theme park, I was thrilled. Something different to tell the folks back home.

The train is filling up now. Lots of people, it seems, are taking the opportunity to visit the new attraction. Most of them, if not all, are Russians, the middle-aged and elderly, families with small children. Everyone in their bright summer clothes, chatting, eating their picnics, *pirozhki*, smoked sausage, cheese and rolls. The old lady opposite me, a regular rosy-cheeked babushka, smiles and nods and offers us some little buns.

'*Kolobki*', she says.

'Name of cake', explains Irina and I smile back at the babushka, taking one out of politeness.

'Tell her it's delicious', I say, munching. Though actually it's too sweet for my taste. More and more people are piling in. We have to squash up on the seat. 'Seems it's a popular destination', I say to Irina, who nods.

'Yes, there is historic interest, of course, and also, for some, nostalgia'.

'Really?'

'Some of our old people don't think things here have changed for the better'.

A whistle blows, a guard outside our window waves a red flag and the train rumbles into motion. I experience that customary fluttering in my stomach at the start of any adventure. The train pulls out of the station. It is going very slowly as we traverse the city, its modern centre with glass skyscrapers squashed up against onion-domed churches, the iconic spires of a couple of Stalin's Seven Sisters, anachronistically gothic, visible in the distance, then out through endless suburbs of apartment blocks and industrial estates. At last we are trundling into the countryside. As I foresaw, the seats aren't at all comfortable, and I fidget a lot. Irina gets up and returns with two glasses of tea, amber-hued without milk, the way they drink it here. Sugar barely masks its bitter flavour.

'How long is the journey?' I ask.

She shrugs. 'Not so long, I think. Russia is big country. Not more certainly than one day'.

'A day!'

She laughs. 'I joke you, David. Look, here we are already at tunnel. On other side is Soviet World'.

We sweep into the tunnel and I glimpse a ghostly reflection in the window, gaunt and hollow-eyed. Do I really look like that? But then suddenly we are engulfed in complete darkness. Like being in a cave when they turn off the electricity to show you what it was like in prehistoric times. I don't like it. I've never liked it. I always need at least a chink of light or I get claustrophobic and panicky. I grip the slats of my seat and close my eyes. The tunnel goes on and on. Suddenly light breaks through my tightened eyelids. I look. I blink, I look again. What the hell! Everything has changed. My fellow travellers, recently so animated, sit dourly upright in dull outfits, predominantly grey and navy and black. They stare at me with hostile suspicion. Of Irina there is no sign at all, which is unfortunate, since she has the tickets and here comes the guard. My fellow travellers proffer their stubs wordlessly.

Then the guard arrives at me. He has a wide pale face, like a boiled suet pudding, and doesn't look at all friendly. I try to explain but my Russian is as non-existent as his English. He starts to yell. Everyone is staring. I get out my passport and show it to him. He snatches it, examines it with a sneer on his face and disappears. Too soon to panic, surely. I wait, staring out of the window at muddy fields, but conscious that all eyes are on me.

At last Irina returns with the guard. I hardly recognise her. She is in some sort of uniform and her lovely hair has been ferociously bleached so that only dark roots are visible. I hope it's a wig. But then maybe the curls were the wig. Her lips are smeared scarlet. But at least she smiles and hands me back my passport.

'Sorry, David. Misunderstanding'.

The guard mutters and moves off about his business.

'But you see', she continues. 'First experience of Soviet World'.

I laugh too, perhaps a bit louder than warranted. I get it now. It was all a set-up, part of the introduction. I smile at the fierce babushka opposite so that she can share the joke, but she just scowls and looks away.

'But how did you do that? How did they? I mean change so quickly?'

'Trade secret', she replies. 'Now, you see', indicating her uniform, 'I am registered Intourist guide'.

We pull into a station. I can't read the Cyrillic alphabet but Irina tells me this is Sovietograd, our destination. The city, or whatever it is, as we walk out into it, is an industrial grey monster of monolithic architecture. I am immediately struck by the absence of advertising hoardings except for those on the tops of buildings or on enormous posters lauding the achievements of communism in hard red. Irina translates: *Long live the heroic Communist Party of the Soviet Union; Glory to worldwide*

October; Every day life is getting better; Be watchful; Counter-revolutionaries threaten our glorious Soviet achievements; Hail to the legacy of Marx and Lenin.

We climb on a rickety tram, already choc-a-bloc with people. Impossible to move, so newcomers pass coins across other passengers' heads to receive their ticket from a machine. Irina does the same.

'We could travel for nothing', I say, and she gives me a look. 'I'm not suggesting it', I add. 'But we could'.

She points to a line of photographs of people pasted above the windows. '*Zaitsy*', she says. 'Hares. People caught riding with no ticket'.

'Ah, name and shame. Horror show'.

My rucksack clearly bothers people and old women grumble around me. I take it off and put it under my feet but apparently that's not the thing either, since I constantly have to move it to let other people pass me to get on or off.

'Do they all actually live here or are they paid actors?' I ask, but the rattling of the tram drowns out my question and Irina shakes her head to indicate she can't hear me.

After an age we arrive at a creepy world of blocky and undifferentiated high rise apartments, all old and in a state of disrepair. Alighting from the tram, we walk through a sandy yard, past a children's playground of faded plaster animals. A solitary infant clambers over a crocodile. The child is so bundled up that his or her shape and face can hardly be discerned – and why it is suddenly so cold? I shiver in my thin jacket, thinking we can't have travelled that far north in such a short space of time.

There's a pinched-faced woman in her late forties sitting nearby with a cigarette, perhaps the grandmother, for she occasionally calls out warnings to the child, 'Alyosha, Alyosha!'

Alyosha. The youngest and sweetest of the Brothers Karamazov. So at least now I know the child is a boy.

Irina leads the way to one of the high rises. She points out the number 43 over the small entrance. 'So you will know it again'.

We climb a dark and filthy staircase that stinks of cooked cabbage. On the second floor she stops outside a heavily padded door. She inserts a key into the lock and opens it. 'Here is where you stay', she says. 'Communal apartment'.

Is it my imagination or has her attitude become more frosty since the train? She certainly isn't laughing as much.

'Communal?'

'How Soviet peoples live. In shared accommodation'.

She gives me two keys, one to the front door and another to my room. As we walk down the corridor, we meet a woman who looks at me with unmasked suspicion and dislike. Irina says something to her but she just grunts in response. I have to say this isn't quite how I imagined it would be, although at the same time I'm not sure what I was expecting. My room is, to speak politely, compact, and packed with furniture: a bed, a couch, a bookcase full of hefty tomes with blue covers, a small table and two chairs. Grubby brown curtains hang on each side of a double-paned window.

'You cook in kitchen', Irina says. 'I show you instantly'.

I put down my rucksack and sit on the bed. It is too soft, sagging in the middle. I worry about my back.

The same unfriendly neighbour is already in the kitchen, roughly chopping onions and lumpy potatoes and putting them in a saucepan. She ignores us. The room features a sticky-looking table, rickety chairs and a gigantic fridge. A wide unsavoury-looking sink. A bucket with a dirty mop in it propped against the green tiled wall.

'Twelve persons live in apartment', Irina tells me. 'You must respect them and take your turn to cook'.

'Ah well, I don't suppose I'll be cooking here', I say. 'I'd like to eat out'.

'Up to you'. She doesn't seem interested. 'Washing machines in basement'.

I laugh. 'Surely I won't be here long enough to do any washing'. It's only a three-day trip, after all, which I am beginning to think will be plenty.

'Ok. So now I show you bathroom'.

This is the biggest shock so far. First the smell. Someone here must have really bad digestive problems. The lavatory bowl is browny-yellow, with accumulated limescale. Clearly no one here has heard of bleach. The handbasin is blotched with black as if someone handling coal has been the last to use it, and the bath is worse, with an acidic green streak down the middle. Mould on the walls. No shower. But Irina takes it all in her stride. This is normal, apparently.

She explains how to get into town on the tram and gives me some Soviet money, notes worn thin and dark, a handful of coins.

'When will I see you again?' I ask, a bit ruefully. Is she really going to abandon me here?

'Tomorrow, for sure. Now rest, explore neighbourhood, whatever you want. Enjoy yourself. Find shops, *stolovaya*'.

'What?'

'*Sto-lo-va-ya*. Restaurant, if you don't want to eat at home'.

Home?

She has gone and I return to my room. A man is sitting on my bed. 'Who are you?' I ask.

He stands up. 'Hi', he replies smiling and in English. 'I am Vitaly, Vitya, your roommate'.

Room-mate. Irina didn't mention that.

Ok, so I'm not too thrilled about sharing a room, though no doubt it's all part of the 'Soviet experience'. However, since Irina seems to have abandoned me to my fate, it's a big advantage meeting someone friendly at last, who speaks English, knows the ropes and can break me in.

My first concern is that there is only one bed in the room.

'No problem', Vitya says. 'I sleep on couch'.

It's a lumpy hairy piece of furniture of a length that would necessitate a reasonably-sized male body curling up into a foetal position, so I don't argue the point with him. After all, I've paid a pretty penny for this excursion.

Then I express the desire to go and eat somewhere. Can Vitya suggest a place?

'There's a place near tram stop', he says. 'We can go there'.

I haven't asked him to join me but am happy for him to come. He's a skinny, lopsided-looking fellow, with hair like greasy straw sticking out round a pale yellow face. Lips rather too red and wet. A mournful expression that lights up when he smiles (shame about those bad teeth), and merry blue eyes, his best feature. Normally I wouldn't be seen dead with anyone who dressed like that, in a cheap patterned sweater and shiny tracksuit bottoms, but hey, I'm on my holidays.

The *stolovaya* isn't so much a restaurant as a canteen. Grubby white-tiled walls and concrete floor, plastic coated tables and metal chairs. We get ourselves trays and join the queue for the self-service counter. Nothing looks particularly appetising but Vitya asks the formidably stout serving woman for the soup. I tell him to get me the same and with a grim expression she thrusts two metal bowls of oily liquid at us. Vitya takes several slabs of black bread and I do the same, along with a small pot of what he says is sour cream. Then he asks the next equally intimidating woman – and what strong red arms they have – for some oval objects, mysteriously disguised with breadcrumbs.

'Rissoles', he tells me.

She has dolloped some sort of brown grain next to them.

'*Kasha*', says Vitya. 'Quite tasty'.

I can't see anything better so I ask for the same and with a big sigh she replicates her previous actions.

Vitya takes a bottle of mineral water at the final counter but I prefer tea, amber and milkless as ever, served in a glass with a surprisingly decorative tin holder, featuring a leaf design curling round an embossed neo-classical building. I have to ask for sugar. Apparently it costs extra.

Vitya insists on treating me to this feast. He gets two chocolates with his change.

'Nice touch', I say.

'No, is instead of kopecks'.

While we are eating – and if I wasn't so hungry I'd abandon both dishes after the first couple of nasty mouthfuls – a bent and aged crone in a stained overall swishes a grey mop resembling Medusa's head under our feet. Next she wipes our table with a stinking rag.

Vitya laughs. 'It is my plan when I go to West to open Soviet restaurant just like this. What you think, David? I make the millions of dollars?'

'When you go to the West?'

'Is my dream one day'.

'But surely you can go now whenever you like. I mean, there are no restrictions any more, are there?'

He looks at me. 'No restrictions?'

'Well of course I understand if it's too expensive'.

'Influence, David. You have to know right people. Or if I had one drop, one little tiny drop of Jew blood. Or, there is old joke: Comrade is asked how would you travel abroad from Soviet Union? Comrade replies, I don't want to travel. I am happy here in communistical paradise. He is asked again, yes but if you had to travel, how would you go? Well, comrade says, question don't arise because I only have internal passport. Asked again: no but all that aside, if they sent you, how would you go? Ah, if they sent me, then of course I would go in a tank'.

He almost falls off his chair laughing.

I am confused. Is he talking to me in character? Is that what they are trained to do here? That must be it. I think suddenly of the film *The Truman Show*, where a whole town with all its inhabitants is built around the one character who doesn't realise it's a fake. I suppose Truman is me except that I know it's fake. Well, anyway, if that's how Vitya wants to or has to play it at the moment, that's ok. For now.

I ask about nightlife and he looks at me for a moment, as if perplexed. 'There are clubs in city centre', he says, 'but ... well, I suppose we could go some place'.

I sense his reluctance and anyway I am suddenly feeling worn out after the travelling, the new impressions and the heavy food. And just can't face that cramped tram ride again. 'Maybe tomorrow', I say, though it seems a waste of a holiday to spend the first evening staying in.

'We can have party in room', smiles Vitya, as if reading my mind.

On leaving the *stolovaya*, he stops at a grocery store to buy a bottle of vodka and other stuff for the evening. There is an elaborate ritual attached to this, it seems, in that it is necessary first of all to queue at the liquor counter and place an order, for which we receive a docket. We then have to queue at another counter to get a docket for smoked sausage and at a third for dill pickles. Then we queue at the cashier's booth to pay for our purchases. This cashier, who looks a bit like the new Irina, all badly bleached hair and smeary red lipstick, speedily calculates the total on an abacus, her fingers whizzing. Then we have to return to all the different counters, queue to present our stamped dockets and receive our items, now wrapped in greaseproof paper (apart from the bottle of vodka). It all seems ridiculously complicated and bureaucratic, as if designed to wear people down, and I say as much to Vitya.

'Normal', he shrugs.

Outside the shop, a man lies on the ground, an almost empty vodka bottle beside him. 'Idiot probably stood here and drank all', Vitya says. 'Without food. Suicide'.

I look down at the prone body. The man lying in the muck with his hectically red face, sparse grey hair and stentorian snoring is a tribute to the care for detail that has gone into the creation of this theme park. I make a mental note to write as much to TripAdvisor when I get back and I whip out my little Canon to take a photo. I take a picture, too, of Vitya, with his lopsided grin, straw hair and string bag. He laughs and asks to see the camera, which I hand to him.

'Nice', he says. 'Digital, yes?'

I nod. 'By the way, let me contribute to the cost of all that'. I gesture to the bag and starts getting out my wallet, but he shakes his head.

'No, David. Today, you are my guest. Tomorrow perhaps you go to Beriozka in centre city to buy with your dollars'.

'Where?'

'Beriozka. Hard currency shop. You can get me cigarettes, not like these filthy *papyrosi*'.

He is smoking something pungent with no filter, just a cardboard tube at the mouth end, like a child's cigarette holder. 'Marlboro or Kent or Camel. All are good'.

Back at the apartment there is no sign of our eleven flatmates, apart from the roar of TVs from behind closed doors. Vitya unlocks our room and looks around.

'Someone has been here', he says.

I am concerned. 'How can you tell?'

'It looks untidy but I leave things a certain way so I can tell if anything has been moved'.

I check my rucksack. 'Nothing missing anyway. Are you sure?'

He shrugs. 'Maybe I make mistake. Or maybe they just look'.

'That's creepy. Does it happen often?'

He makes a face. 'Is normal'.

I am sceptical but say nothing. Meanwhile he is putting the vodka bottle out on the window ledge to chill. 'If I put it in fridge in kitchen it will be stolen. They are all thieves in this apartment. Thieves and spies'.

I am amused. 'Spies?'

'They say that one in four of population is spy. There are twelve people living here. Do the math, David'.

He puts on the TV. A serious-looking man is pontificating about what I have no idea. Vitya changes the channel. Another serious-looker pontificating equally seriously. On the next channel, a man is hunched over a desk reading from a page. He looks haunted and I am sure those are bruises on his face.

'What's going on there?'

'Nothing. Rubbish'. Vitya is lighting another of those horrible cigarettes but since it's really his room, I don't feel I can do more than cough. He doesn't take the hint.

'No, but what is it?'

'Nothing. Some stupid confession'.

'About what?'

'Who knows. Maybe he steal money. Maybe he is black-marketeer. Maybe he betrays Motherland. Maybe he is spy for your West'.

'And they broadcast it?'

'Of course. So people will know'.

I look again at the man's face. Isn't there something familiar about it? Vitya quickly switches channel again to one where a band of musicians is accompanying a singer with a gravelly voice.

'Soviet jazz', says Vitya contemptuously but leaves it on loud. 'Now no one hears what we say'.

'Who would be listening?'

'They listen, I assure you my friend. They listen'. He waved his hand at the light fixtures, the wall plugs, anywhere a microphone could be hidden.

'But why would they bother? I'm only a tourist and you, Vitya, well forgive me but you don't look very threatening'.

'Whole country suffering from paranoia, David. Is illness. Is under our skins'. Vitya is whispering and I do the same although I know that any self-respecting surveillance device these days will be able to separate out our speech from the background noise. 'Remember', my room-mate continues, 'how you ask me in *stolovaya* about my military service. Immediately I am thinking, why he asks this question. He is spy?'

'For God's sake, I was only making conversation'.

'I know, but at same time, you see, I am infected too, so I suspect'.

Which no doubt is why he reckoned the room had been entered in our absence.

'I won't ask any more personal questions, I promise'.

'No, just ask about military installations, nuclear power plants, dissident groups. I tell you all you want to know'. He laughs.

'Dissident groups?'

'People who want same freedom you have in West. To criticise system, to express themselves freely through art and literature without dead hand of academy, to travel, even to buy nice things. You have nice things, David. Your jeans …'

Well, I agree, they are rather nice. And very expensive. *True Religion* designer brand.

'Maybe you give them to me when you leave'.

'Maybe', I say. In your dreams, Vitya.

'If you want, I can introduce you'.

'Who to?'

'Some dissidents. I know them'.

'Yes, well, that would be interesting, I suppose'.

'Tomorrow, we can do that'.

'Don't you have to go to work?'

He laughs, showing those teeth. 'No personal questions, David, remember'.

When I wake up in the early hours on that too soft bed, my head is throbbing. I vaguely remember the hours before, the vodka drunk too quickly as we proposed ever more ridiculous toasts to each other: to me, to Vitya, to universal brotherhood, to Lenin, to Stalin, to Margaret Thatcher (still much admired here it seems among certain groups), to the stout woman in the *stolovaya*, to the old crone who cleaned our table with her filthy rag, to Vitya's restaurant in the West, to Irina …

'Irina?' he'd asked.

'My guide'.

'Your guide. I thought that was me?'

'My official Intourist guide'.

'So where is she, this guide? Let her come here and party … Irinochka … Oh, my God, vodka all gone. How that happen?'

It was true, the bottle was empty.

'Wait', he said and left the room, opening and shutting the door very quietly. In a few moments, he was back with another bottle.

'Where did you get that?' I asked.

'No personal questions, please'. And he winked, raising a full glass. 'To the beautiful Irinochka'.

'To Irina'.

Later I remember hearing an eerie call rising from in the yard outside the apartment.

'What's going on?' I asked.

'They are asking for the third man'.

'The third man? Like in the film?'

Vitya looked puzzled. 'No. What film? ... You see, David, this is how it goes. Three men buy one bottle and share. Is enough to get nicely drunk'. He laughed and poured more from our second bottle. '*Na zdarovye*!' We'd clinked glasses and knocked it back. And after that I have no memory at all.

I need the bathroom now and stumble out of bed. There's a dim light in the hallway so I can find my way without accidentally wandering into someone else's room. The bathroom smells if anything even more disgusting than before, especially after I throw up in the lavatory bowl. When I pull the flush it is as if a mighty waterfall comes crashing down. Surely it will wake up the whole flat.

But the same silence accompanies me back down the passageway and I suddenly wonder if all these actors have real homes to go to and only appear during their working hours. I am tempted to try and peek in one of the rooms but just as my hand lands on the doorknob a tremendous snore from the other side convinces me of the folly of the enterprise as well as its pointlessness, now that I know someone is actually there.

When I open our door, Vitya is briefly illuminated, stretched out on the couch, bony yellow feet dangling off the edge. He seems to be fast asleep. I on the other hand now feel wide awake, thoughts and impressions buzzing round in my head. Particularly exercising me is the question of what is real here and what isn't and I determine to have it out with Vitya in the morning.

After all, I must have fallen back into sleep because I wake up with my roommate hanging over me, fully dressed.

'How you feel, comrade?' he asks.

'Not too bad, considering', I reply, but when I try to get up, my head thuds like a Lambeg drum.

'Here', Vitya says, offering a concoction in a glass. 'Swallow it down quick'.

I sniff it. 'Ugh, what is it?'

'Pickle juice. Guaranteed to cure'.

'My God!'

'Drink', he orders and I do, spluttering at the acidity of it. Not sure if it cures my head but it certainly distracts from the pain.

'When you are able, get up and we go downtown'.

I remember Irina. She said she'd see me today. I tell Vitya this.

'Would be nice, of course, but when she come?'

I don't know.

'So we sit around all day waiting for this woman? No. Better let her find you'.

This makes sense so I give myself a rudimentary wash, not to spend any more time than necessary in that bathroom, with the stench of my own vomit from last night still contributing to the general aromatic cocktail. Then, without breakfast – in any case there's nothing to eat here except last night's leavings, some half-chewed sausage and black bread – Vitya and I head off to the tram.

It's a crisp morning and lots of people are hurrying in the same direction as we are. There's a long queue at the stop and when the tram arrives it's already full. No one is put off by this and people start to pile on.

'Should we wait for the next one?' I ask.

Vitya shakes his head. 'Will be same'. And on he goes, pulling me after him.

I am squashed against a little old woman and a young man in a fake leather jacket. Despite the intimacy of our proximity, neither acknowledges my presence.

The journey, as they say, seems endless. I try to sublimate but it's hard, especially when the tram swings around a corner and I am pushed up against one or the other of my companions in torment, the old woman's cushiony breasts, the young man's slippery slickness. And then there are the people who push past us to get on or off. Or who pass their coins over our heads to the ticket machine that they themselves have no hope of ever reaching. I presume Vitya has organised ours for both of us. I hope so. I don't want another encounter with a guard. Or to have my mugshot displayed on the inside of the tram. Finally we tumble off into what looks to be a main square. Blind-eyed buildings loom around it, while in the middle stands a heroic statue of Lenin pointing at the Diamond Hotel, a misnomer if ever there was one for such a heavy block of concrete. However, I find myself wondering about the quality of its bathrooms.

Vitya tells me he isn't allowed in the hotel, which is only for foreigners. A muscle-bound doorman studies me when I walk in, looks at the designer jeans and says nothing. To the right of the lobby is the Beriozka shop. Vitya says the name means birch tree. Nice.

I take a metal basket and check out the shelves. What a contrast to the grocery I was in yesterday. This shop is packed with Western goodies, whisky, gin, cognac, liqueurs, as well as Russian vodka and champagne,

Georgian wine. I select a couple of bottles of Stolichnaya and a bottle of the single malt Scotch I like. I add a carton of Marlboro, wondering what Vitya would say if I told him the Marlboro man died of lung cancer. There are food items too and I chuck in a small jar of caviar for the craíc. The haul isn't cheap but my American Express does nicely, thank you. Or *'Spacibo'*, as the highly groomed and heavily made up young woman at the counter says to me, lifting dark eyes and gazing into mine.

Outside the shop, in the lobby, I am accosted by another beauty who asks me for the time, and when I check my watch (an Invicta, not cheap), asks me if I have the time to buy her a drink. I tell her my wife is waiting for me to which she replies in that slithery accent, 'too bad. Maybe later, darling, when wife is not waiting'.

'So how come', I ask Vitya outside, 'she can go in the hotel and you can't?'

'My innocent in abroad', he replies, slapping my shoulder. 'She pays bribe to doorman out of earnings. In fact, doorman probably her pimp'.

'You mean she wasn't interested in my sparkling personality, only the contents of my wallet'.

Vitya is in high spirits and lights up one of the new cigarettes straight away. I decide not to tell him about the Marlboro man.

'Now what you want to see?' he asks.

'What's worth seeing?'

'Nothing'. He laughs. 'Maybe you should go for drink with party girl'.

'Well', I say. 'I wouldn't mind some breakfast'.

'My God, you are right. We haven't eaten yet. I forget. Let's go to café'.

We pass quite a few before Vitya decides on one he likes the look of. Me, I am increasingly bewildered. This is indeed a whole city, buzzing with life. Nothing like any theme park I've ever been in before. But I think I have sussed the explanation, bizarre though it is. Instead of building on a greenfield site, they have simply requisitioned for tourism purposes a typical Soviet city. Possibly on a certain level, everything ticks on as usual: people go to work, children go to school. I wonder, however, what the inhabitants think about having to live under such oppressive conditions. I hope they are well rewarded. They are certainly into method acting. Even when drunk, Vitya refused to open up to me on the subject. Playing dumb. Maybe I'll have better luck with him today.

In the café there's a group of people that Vitya knows. He introduces me and then they start talking animatedly in Russian. I feel a bit left out at first until he turns to me and says that the tall intense man, introduced as Seryozha, is an artist, in fact one of the very dissidents he had been thinking of the previous day.

'What a coincidence!'

'Yes, indeed'.

I've never been much of a believer in coincidences but I'm happy to go with the flow.

'You want to see his studio. Just near'.

'Why not'.

This time Vitya lets me pay the bill for the whole group, which, apart from Seryozha, includes his girlfriend Masha and another couple, Dima and Lyuba. The girls are friendly but Dima disconcerts, with his dark silence and habit of spitting whenever I say anything.

We leave the café and go round the corner to a high building faced in the yellow stucco that is characteristic of this older part of the city. The studio is on the top floor and there is no lift. I am out of breath and gasping by the time we get to the top.

It's a big room but choc-a-bloc with stacked paintings and an easel featuring Seryozha's latest oeuvre, a violently-hued nude, that to me resembles the victim of some terrible attack, twisted limbs, dead face. I am shown one after another of variations on this theme and I make what I think are appropriately appreciative noises when suddenly I become aware of five pairs of expectant eyes fixed on me and realise they are hoping I will buy something.

'You know', I say. 'I really don't know anything about modern art. And also they're too big for my tiny apartment'.

The artist looks at me with disdain as if I have been wasting his precious time. I mean, he could have had another cup of coffee at my expense in the café.

'Show him your drawings, Seryozha', says Vitya, ever optimistic, and a huge portfolio is lugged out from behind some paintings. I sigh inwardly. It seems I won't get away without parting from more money. It also turns out – when I have selected a small, scratchy sketch of exactly what I am not sure, a torso, a tree, a pillar – that roubles are not acceptable here and that I must dip into my small and precious hoard of dollars, since Seryozha doesn't take American Express. But at least geniality has been restored and a bottle of vodka is brought out to clinch the deal. I protest it's too early to drink but apparently this won't do. Form demands the tossing back of a glass although I refuse absolutely more than one.

'Well', says Vitya, shaking the Beriozka bag so that the bottles clink. 'We can have party later'.

There follows an exchange in rapid Russian. Vitya turns to me. 'I have something to discuss with the guys. Mashenka and Lyubochka would like to show you some of our city, if you agree. Then we can meet for lunch back here later'.

They are both pretty girls, so I put up no resistance. In fact, I am glad to get away from Seryozha as well as the silent, sullen Dima, who makes me feel uneasy.

'We go to park', says Masha. 'It is nice there'.

There's a chill in the air but it isn't unpleasant. We walk briskly enough and the circulation gets going. The park runs alongside a murky river but we take a tree-lined path towards a fountain visible in the distance. Heroic marching songs blare from loudspeakers along the way. The fountain, when we reach it, features massively muscled heroic workers apparently striding together towards a golden dawn, pouring water out of buckets and hoses in a constant pointless stream.

'Is by one of our most famous Soviet sculptures', Masha tells me. We look at it.

'You like?'

'Actually, I think it's pretty horrible', I say.

The girls look confused. 'Pretty or horrible?'

'Horrible'.

They laugh. 'So David, is true you really don't like so much the modern art', says Lyuba.

'Not really, no'.

'But ancient art, you like that'.

'Ancient art?'

'Like for example icons'.

'Oh ... yes, of course. Very much'.

'Here near park is church with nice icons. You want to see?'

'That sounds good'.

We come to a small white building with onion domes painted blue and sprinkled with stars. It is in a state of disrepair but I take a photo all the same. Masha tells me it is one of the few churches in the city still operating as such.

'In Great Patriotic War it was used to store the grains', Lyuba adds, 'but now church again'.

Old women sit outside, as well as injured soldiers, missing legs, arms and eyes: horrible injuries that surely couldn't be faked. And again I ask myself, what sort of theme park is this at all? The air inside the church is so heavy with incense it's hard to breathe. There are no seats and people just wander around. A woman has prostrated herself on the floor and we have to step carefully over her. I notice all the women here are wearing scarves on their heads. Even Masha and Lyuba. Masha buys a candle.

'You are religious?' I ask.

She laughs. 'I am … what is word, Lyubochka?' She says it in Russian.

'She is superstitious'.

'Yes, I am super …' She lights her candle and places it in front of an icon of the Madonna and child. 'Beautiful yes?'

'Very'. It is, even though the gold halos once round the Virgin's head and that of the baby have been removed.

'You like to buy it?'

'What? Buy it?'

So am I in a shop now?

Lyuba smiles. 'Not this one', she says. 'One like it. Small. Can fit in your bag. Hang on wall of tiny apartment'.

Is she laughing at me?

'Talk outside', says Masha, looking round. 'Who knows who listens'.

One in four a spy, I think. Outside, I fish a note from my wallet and proffer it to the most abject-looking of the soldiers.

'Are you mad?' says Masha, snatching it out of my hand. 'Too much. Kopecks will do for him'.

So kopecks it is but I am conscious of his one yellow eye, the eyes of everyone on us as we run the gauntlet of the beggars.

'They should be moved off', says Lyuba. 'Is terrible to see such things'.

Once away from the church, it seems the girls have decided to abandon chit-chat and get down to business.

'You like such an icon. We can get it for you'.

'You mean a copy'.

'No, no, no. Real ancient icon, it belongs to our auntie. Not Andrey Rublyov, of course, but genuine masterpiece'.

I have to say I am tempted. What would the folk back home have to say about that? 'Wouldn't it cost a fortune? We Westerners aren't all millionaires, you know'.

'Not so very much money. Few hundred'.

'Roubles or dollars?'

They both find that immensely funny. 'Dollars, of course'.

'I'm sorry, I didn't bring that sort of money with me. Buying Seryozha's picture has virtually cleaned me out'.

That expression I have to explain. The girls talk to each other animatedly in Russian, with much waving of arms.

'You have credit card, yes?' asks Masha.

'Well, yes ...'

'So this is what we do. We give list. You buy stuff for us in Beriozka. Luxury goods. We make exchange. Horror show?'

'Great idea, yes', says Lyuba, smiling and taking my hand. Hers is soft and warm. She's prettier than Masha and her eyes seems to offer an invitation that no red-blooded man could refuse.

'I'd have to see the picture ... and think about it'.

'Of course'. They are very happy now.

And I haven't committed myself to anything. Not yet.

But the girls aren't going to let any grass grow under their feet. It seems we are going straight to Auntie's apartment. By tram. I have to say, however, that jiggling up against Lyuba is by no means an unpleasant experience. Our faces, not to mention the rest of our bodies, are very close together. Her hair smells nice, clean and lightly perfumed. I am only marginally taller than she in her high-heeled boots and when she turns her face towards me I could oh so easier lean forward and kiss her. I wonder is gloomy Dima really her boyfriend, or just a friend? They hadn't seemed particularly close when I saw them together. But when I ask, she just laughs. The tip of her pink tongue licks a pinker top lip. If she presses any closer against me, she will soon find out how I feel about her. We finally get off the tram into another concrete forest of high-rises. Auntie, it turns out, lives in a communal apartment just like mine, sharing her room with a big lout of a teenage son who stares wordlessly at us from the couch. The girls explain the purpose of our visit and Auntie, a heavy woman with a scarf tied peasant-fashion round her face, lumbers off into a recess made with a curtain, presumably some attempt at privacy.

She returns with a small, rather dirty image of the crucifixion painted on wood. The stylised face of a weary Christ peers at me through cracks in the paint. Its poor condition however simply convinces me of its authenticity. I pull a face to indicate my disappointment, to conceal the excitement I feel inside.

'It's not great', I say. 'How much does she want for it?'

There are some mumblings and then Masha names a ridiculously high sum.

I shake my head. 'Not possible', I say, making to hand the icon back.

'So how much? How much?'

Now I've bargained all over the place – North Africa, the Middle East, Turkey – and consider myself good at it. I am only slightly put off my stroke by the steady stare of the loutish son. But maybe he's just mentally deficient. Auntie predictably rejects my first offer but gradually we proceed to an agreement, only slightly more than I had intended to spend. The icon will be mine.

It is by now way past lunchtime and we jiggle back on the tram to the city centre, this time with Lyuba clutching the plastic bag containing the icon well wrapped in old copies of *Pravda*. I am wondering if the next stop will be the Beriozka but apparently not. Tomorrow, my last full day, will be the occasion for that visit. I am glad of it. I can sleep on the decision and if necessary change my mind.

At the studio the men have been knocking back my single malt whiskey. They haven't prepared any lunch and Lyuba and Masha immediately go to the kitchen. I offer to help and they all look at me as if I am mad. It's women's work in this society apparently, and they laugh loudly when I insist that I enjoy cooking.

Instead I find I am expected to catch up with the other men in the drinking marathon. We toast my new purchase, which has to be unwrapped and admired. A toast to Lyuba and Masha, a toast to universal friendship, to world peace, to New York, to London, Paris and Rome.

By now, my Glenfiddich is all gone and we have started on the first bottle of Stolichnaya and still no sign of anything to eat. I only had a small roll for breakfast back in the café and feel the drink go straight to my head. After all my resolutions to stay sober, as well. But at least the drink has loosened tongues, particularly Dima's.

'David'. He puts his arm around my shoulders. 'Do you know what is Russian soul?'

'I've heard of it'.

'Russian soul ... we ... how to say it ... we love to suffer. Have you read Dostoyevsky? *Crime and Punishment. Man from Underground*'. I nod. 'Have you heard of *Klysti*?'

'Er …'

'Religious fanatics who beat themselves till blood runs. *Skoptsi* who cut off their menhood. *Dukhabors* who take off all clothses and burn houses to show how they hate materials'. He is clutching me very tightly. He has steel-capped teeth and bad breath. Vitya crosses over to us with a kitchen knife.

'Here, Dima. If you want, cut off menhood'.

They are laughing maniacally. Me too. The room swims around us. Or we swim in the room. In vodka.

'But I am most serious', Dima continues, 'Soviet Union symptom of our suffering. We love Stalin because he beats us and kills us. Because we hate ourselves. Because we deserve to suffer'.

Suddenly Masha screams out, '*Raskayaniye*! Repentance!' And falls to her knees. She has been drinking as well.

'But listen', I manage to stutter. 'All this … all this …'

'Yes, David. All this … ha ha ha …'

'It's all fake, isn't it? All made up. No more Soviet Union. The wall came down in '89'.

There's a sudden silence. Then they all laugh even harder.

'You know that', I say. 'You're all actors, aren't you. Pretending to be dissidents, like the guard on the train, the bouncer at the hotel, pretend to be hard men. Irina in her Intourist uniform. It's all part of the show I paid to come to see'.

They are looking at me now like I am some sort of maniac. Or maybe it's just bad form to rip down the scenery and expose the mechanisms.

'You paid to see show in Sovietograd?' says Vitya. 'My friend, they robbed you'. And they all laugh again like hyenas round a carcass.

Lyuba fills my glass to the top. She puts a piece of herring in my mouth. I can smell the fish on her fingers. I can smell her hair.

'I have good idea', she says. 'Let's play *Dukhobors* and take off all our clothses'.

She starts unbuttoning my shirt.

I wake up on the floor entwined with someone, Lyuba. We are naked. I don't recall making love. I don't recall anything. I open my eyes and see Masha and Seryozha on the couch, also naked. Vitya is slumped in a corner, fully clothed. He seems to be asleep but I catch a glint from an eye that isn't completely shut. Of Dima there's no sign.

I am dying of thirst. Must have a drink. I extricate myself from Lyuba and stagger to the bathroom, naked as I am. Too bad if I meet a neighbour. Even though the guidebooks say not to drink the tap water, I guzzle it down. Someone enters. It is Masha. Unselfconsciously she sits on the lavatory and pees. Then sighs, stands and stretches her arms above her head. I can't stop myself staring at her breasts. I've never seen any like them, massive bulbs that hang down over a flat belly. She sees me looking, lifts one breast and offers it to me.

I must still have been drunk. Never, not even in Thailand, have I done such things.

'We must now go to Beriozka', Lyuba is saying over breakfast, rolls fetched by Vitya from a nearby bakery, with very welcome, very strong coffee. No one has mentioned the night-time goings on, and I'm definitely not going to bring up the subject.

I have been thinking about it all, however, and have come to a disturbing conclusion. Or perhaps that's too strong. A theory. I am starting to suspect that the inhabitants here have no idea they are living in a theme park. Perhaps, like the mother in *Goodbye Lenin*, the fall of communism has been kept a secret from them in case they all drop dead from shock. They are living in a prelapsarian bubble, so to speak. I decide to test the theory.

'Have you ever been to Moscow?' I ask Lyuba. She shakes her head.

'I dream of it, of course, like Chekhov's three sisters. But more, I dream of New York, London, Paris'.

'Really'.

'Dreams are permitted, yes?'

The tip of that pink tongue again runs back and forth across her top lip, distracting me.

The plan is that Lyuba will accompany me to the hard currency shop and pick out what she wants me to buy in exchange for the icon.

'How will you get past the bouncer?'

'As your girlfriend. If I am with you, they won't stop me. Now I get ready'.

She and Masha go off somewhere giggling. Seryozha is still asleep on the couch and Vitya is very quiet. Have I offended him, I wonder? I think of expressing my new theory to him, but he doesn't look as if he would welcome conversation. Perhaps Irina is the one to ask when I finally track her down. I help myself to another roll.

Lyuba reenters after a while, looking like a whore; too much make-up, too short skirt, too low blouse (though her breasts are much smaller and neater than Masha's), fuck-me shoes. I suppose that's the idea. A street woman picked up by the foreign tourist.

The tram is surprisingly empty and we can sit on the hard seats. Lyuba crosses her legs and her skirt rises to the top of her thighs. A babushka opposite stares disapprovingly. Lyuba laughs and bites my ear. The babushka mutters something, a curse maybe.

When we get off in the main square, Lyuba, perhaps remembering her role as guide at last, points out some buildings supposedly of interest. The only one I pay much attention to is the KGB headquarters on the square opposite the Diamond Hotel, a block about five storeys high.

'They say it extends as far underground as above it', Lyuba whispers.

'Here, I say, 'I'll take a picture of you with it in the background'.

She laughs. 'If they see us they arrest us'.

'No, no. I am just a stupid tourist taking a picture of my girl'.

'Am I your girl?'

'Of course'.

'And Masha?'

'Masha is Seryozha's girl', I look at her steadily. Masha must have told her. 'Isn't that right?' I snap her and show her the image.

'My mamma wouldn't recognise me'. She takes my arm and laughs. 'Maybe you marry me, David, and take me to West'.

I laugh too.

'No, really', she says. 'People do it. Business arrangement. How much you charge for that, David? How much?'

'A lot', I say laughing too. 'Too much'.

She looks into my eyes. 'By the way, David, are you Jew?'

'No'.

'Ah?'

'What?'

'Well in Russia name David is for Jews. So I think that yes, you are. But then you like icon and last night I noticed …' She smiled.

'What?'

'Down there'. She lightly tipped my crotch. 'You are not Jew'.

I drive my nails into my palm. Trying to think of something boring. 'Would you like me better if I were Jewish?'

'No, no. Not at all. I cannot like you better than I do'. She laughs. 'So now, let us go in hotel'.

It's a different bouncer, I think, but equally muscular. He says something in Russian to Lyuba and she replies at length. He shrugs, nods and lets us in. Inside I am aghast at her shopping list. It seems I am expected to shell out way more than our original agreement.

'But we have to have the commission', she says teasingly. 'Masha and me'. She pours over the jewellery stand and particularly admires some amber earrings mounted in silver. 'Oh, I love them'. They are absurdly expensive. 'I be so so so grateful'. She rubs herself against me.

'Not here', I say, embarrassed, although the saleswoman seems only interested in her nails.

'Why not?' She looks deep into my eyes. 'You know my name Lyubov. It means "love"'. Her voice is husky. 'I love you, David. Do you love me?'

'Well …'

She laughs at my embarrassment. 'No, you don't love Lyuba. But you like … Yes?'

'Very much'.

'So we can take room here for an hour. How nice would it be?

'Surely that's not possible'.

'I already ask doorman. Bottle of cognac for him. Room for us'.

I am thinking less of the sex than of the room, a firm bed, clean sheets, an ensuite. And then perhaps the sex. What the hell, I'm on holiday. I add a bottle of cognac to the trolley.

'Don't forget earrings'.

We fall in the door grabbing at each other.

'Rape me, David', she whispers, biting my ear.

'What?'

'I like rough. Rape me. Please'.

So she likes rough, does she? Then I'll give her rough. I throw her on the bed. She isn't wearing any panties.

She cries out and I slap her round. 'Horror show', she says softly.

Afterwards, we rest for a bit, then shower and have sex again, under the running water, slow sensuous sex standing up. I never knew I had that much stamina before. Maybe it's these irresistible Russian women. Or maybe she put something in my morning tea.

Afterwards Lyuba stays in the shower to wash her hair and treat her body to the creams and oils the hotel provides. I get back into bed, between cool clean sheets. After what I have been enduring recently, it's luxury, even with the cold eye of Lenin staring across the bed at me from his picture on the wall. To think he was there all the time, watching us.

I fall asleep to the sound of running water. At first a soothing pitter-patter, it gets louder and heavier, eventually thundering down in a deluge. I open my eyes and realise someone is banging on the door.

For a few moments I have trouble remembering where I am, who I am. The hammering continues, along with shouts, helping me focus. Sovietograd, the Diamond Hotel ... I ease myself out of bed, still feeling groggy. I am naked and search for my underpants and jeans. The pants I find but the jeans are nowhere to be seen, only a manky pair of tracksuit bottoms. I can't get my head around this but put them on anyway. There's an old white t-shirt as well, in place of my dark blue Hollister, and I am just pulling this over my head when the door bursts open. The men are wearing uniforms and point guns at me. They start yelling in Russian. Clearly a case of mistaken identity but they look to be in earnest and I put my hands up.

'Lyuba', I say, suddenly remembering and looking round the room. There is no sign of her. Maybe she is in the ensuite having another shower.

'Passport, passport', one of the men shouts, prodding me in the stomach with his gun. But my jacket is gone, with my passport in it. Everything is gone, my clothes, my camera, my watch, the Beriozka bag with all my purchases. Suddenly I grin.

'Another Soviet World Experience', I say, but the prodding man hits me across the mouth, still shouting. Enough, I think. I paid good money but not for this.

'Hey!' I start to say, but am seized from behind, arms locked into handcuffs and manhandled out of the room. Despite all the noise, none of the other hotel guests have ventured out of their rooms to see what's happening, but in the lobby the staff stare at me with disgust. I search out the doorman who gave us the room and there he is. I call across to him but he turns away. Maybe it isn't the right man. These hunks of beefcake all look the same. Outside I am bundled into a black car and driven a short distance to a carpark with an underground entrance. I know where I am. The KGB headquarters I so merrily photographed only a couple of hours earlier.

The man who interviews me is thin as a snake with a too big black suit on him. He looks hungry. Perhaps I'm his dinner, I think, trying to keep up my spirits. But of course this will all be sorted soon and perhaps then we can enjoy a good laugh together, though I am revising my message to TripAdvisor. That blow drew blood.

There is an interpreter too, but I come to suspect by his reactions to what I say that my interrogator knows English very well though concealing this for his own reasons.

I explain that I am a tourist, visiting the Soviet World Experience.

'Some experience so far', I say, grinning. The two men look back, expressionless.

'My guide, Irina, can explain everything'.

'What Irina?'

I suddenly realise I have no idea what her last name is and have no way of contacting her. All my papers have gone. At least I can tell them where I am staying.

The interrogator narrows his already narrow eyes. He asks questions through the interpreter.

'Why you in hotel if you have room in communal apartment? Why you stay in communal apartment? Anyway is forbidden for tourists? You are spy, yes, masquerading as simple stupid tourist. Who you spy for?'

The questions go on and on. For hours it seems. The same ones over and over. Sometimes one or other of the men leave the room briefly, while the one who remains fixes me with a cold eye. I am dying for a drink of water but the snake tells the interpreter to inform me I'll only get food and water when I answer his questions satisfactorily.

'You see, we know how you lie'.

'I'm not lying', I shout. 'Ask Vitya'.

'Ah yes, this Vitya you say is roommate … Well, I have to tell you, David, that Lyudmila Stepanovna says there is no such person. You are in room on your own'.

'Who the hell is Lyudmila …'

'Lives in apartment. She says only you are there'.

'Well, she's lying'.

'Lyudmila Stepanovna has excellent character for telling truth'.

Ah, she's their informant, I realise, guessing she must be the sour-faced woman I saw when I arrived.

'Well, she must at least have seen Irina, when Irina first brought me to the place'.

'But you don't know name or patronymic of this woman. Or won't tell us'.

'She works for Intourist'.

'Is this her?'

A photograph is slapped down in front of me, a dumpy, middle-aged woman.

'No. I've never see this person before'.

'This only Irina working for Intourist in Sovietograd'.

And so it goes on.

Hours more pass and I can't take any more. A guard leads me out into the corridor and down into the depths of the building. Lyuba was right, it extends far below street level. I am thrown into a small cell with a mattress on the floor and no other furniture except a bucket, the purpose of which is obvious since it hasn't been emptied since the last occupant left. A tin cup presumably containing water and a hard crust of bread on a tin plate stand on the floor beside the mattress. I just have time to take all this in when the door slams shut behind me and the room is plunged into total blackness. Is it common practice or do they somehow know of my phobia? I think of *1984* and the rats.

But perhaps after a while my eyes will adjust to the dark and find even the faintest crack of light to provide relief. Round the door frame. Is there? Is there? Nothing.

I pound the door. My screams must bring someone. They must ... Someone must hear me. After a while I subside to the floor. I wrap my arms round my head and try to control my breathing. Perhaps a drink will help. I feel around for the water and knock over the cup. When I lift it there are only a few drops left. I start to sob.

The door opens, dazzling me. I am roughly hauled to my feet and dragged out into the corridor, back to an interrogation room, maybe the same one, grey walls still spattered with some sinisterly dark brown liquid, the same metal table and chairs, the bare bright light bulb swinging in the draught caused by the door opening. But it could also be a different room.

A new interrogator sits there. A fatter, swarthier man in a tight suit. There's no interpreter but the uniformed guard – formidably muscled, with a shaven head and blank face – stays in the room, standing beside the door.

'So David', the interrogator says kindly. 'You have rested'.

I raise astonished eyes to look at him. 'Rested?'

'Fed and watered, I hope'.

'I spilt the water'.

'Oh, very sorry to hear it. Mitya …' and then something in Russian. The guard leaves the room. The interrogator looks at me with twinkling eyes.

'I am Boris Daniilovich, David. I think we can get to bottom of this stupid business quickly, yes'.

Mitya returned with two bottles of mineral water, one for me and one for Boris Daniilovich. I lack the strength even to open the bottle and the interrogator has to do it for me. It tastes sulphurous but at least is thirst quenching. When I have finished it, Boris Daniilovich pushes his bottle towards me as well.

'If you need it', he says.

'Why all this?' I ask. 'I have done nothing'.

'Ah … well now … That's a big claim. *I have done nothing*. Which of us can honestly say that?' He smiles in a friendly way. A canine flashes gold.

I am not in the mood for a philosophical discussion on guilt, but at least, I suppose, the man is cordial. Room for hope in that.

'You see, David', he continues, 'we have the problem. Hotel ...'

I've explained about the hotel, over and over. I've told them everything already – well, nearly everything – about Vitya and Seryozha and Lyuba and Dima and Masha and the icon. I tell it again.

'You are planning to smuggle out historical artwork'. He makes a note on the pad in front of him.

'Not smuggle. I bought it from Lyuba's Auntie. It was to be paid for with stuff from the Beriozka'.

Boris Daniilovich lifts shaggy eyebrows and makes another note.

'I know it sounds like an odd arrangement, but you see I didn't bring enough cash in with me. They'll remember at the Beriozka. They'll have my American Express details'.

'Yes, of course. They have those exact details. They say how you came in with prostitutka, buy expensive gifts, bribe doorman to have room ... He has been punished already by the way...'

'She wasn't a prostitute. It was Lyuba. A friend'.

'This is her?'

Boris Daniilovich takes a photograph out of a folder in front of him and pushes it across the desk to me. It's the picture I took in the square with the KGB building behind her.

'My camera. You must have found it'. Boris Daniilovich inclined his head. 'Where?'

'For now, David, it is I who ask questions. You claim this is your good friend Lyuba, yes?'

'Yes'.

'And she is not a prostitutka?'

I can see why he would think that, the pose, the clothes, the sheer tartiness of her.

'She dressed like that to get into the hotel'.

'Ah, I see. So where is she now, this good friend of yours?'

That's the question. 'I don't know. I thought she was sound but maybe after all she is just a thief'. There's a sob in my voice I can't control. 'Maybe they all are. They even took my clothes. These', I had recognised what I was wearing, 'are Vitya's. I'd never ever wear such things'.

'Ok, so let's say she isn't a prostitutka. Just thief. But then there is more problems. Please listen to this, Mitya ...'

The guard steps forward and places a cassette recorder on the table. Boris Daniilovich switches it on. I almost pass out from shock. It's a recording of Lyuba and me having sex, rough sex. Her screams and cries for help, my orders and threats.

'You don't understand', I say. 'It was a game. She asked me to do that. I wouldn't really force a woman ... And in any case, how did you get the recording?'

'You ask so many questions, David? Ok, I explain you this. Sometimes you must understand in this dangerous world, we have to protect our society against its enemies. So we ... what is the word ... bugger ...? No', he laughs. 'Bug, isn't it. We bug the rooms for security reasons. You understand'.

I remember how Vitya played loud jazz to drown our voices. Not paranoid then, after all.

But now I have reason to hope. This extreme monitoring can surely work in my favour. 'So then if you play the rest of the tape you will hear how after the ... the sex we are good friends. In fact, we go into the shower and make love again'.

'Make love?'

'Yes, well ...'

'Ok. Let's listen … '

The tape runs out. He turns it over but on the other side is only raucous pop music. He looks at me.

'I'm telling the truth', I say.

'Truth is good. Truth is very very good. But I am sorry to say it, David. I don't think you tell me truth'.

He takes more photos out of the folder. I don't recognise them. They aren't mine. Close-ups of blueprints, some of what looks like some sort of a military installation.

'I've never seen any of them before'.

'And yet they are on your camera'.

'I can't explain it. Unless Lyuba took them to incriminate me. Where did you find the camera?'

'Under bed in hotel. She didn't take it when she ran away from you. Ran in fear of life … '

'No, it wasn't like that'.

'Ok. For moment but tell me then how did these pictures get on your camera if you didn't take them?'

'I don't know. Some time when I was asleep, maybe. You have to believe me. I have no idea what those pictures are or where they came from'.

Boris Daniilovich leans back in his chair and fixes me with eyes that aren't twinkling any more.

I have to admit it looks bad. If I were him I'd think me guilty as hell, too. Suddenly I get an idea.

'Listen, what if I take you to the studio. Then I can confront them'.

He thinks about it.

'What is address?'

'I don't know that, but I'm sure I can find it. It's only a short tram ride away, in the older part of the city'.

Boris Daniilovich leans forward and puts a soft and clammy hand over mine.

'You know, David, I like you. I am sorry for you. I think maybe you … how you say … get in deep water over your head …'

I feel myself dangerously near breaking down and keep trying to tell myself, none of this is real. It's play-acting, isn't it?

Boris Daniilovich is still speaking.

'My colleague, who interviewed you first time, he says this man is counter-revolutionary imperialist rat and must feel full force of Soviet justice. Full force. You understand what that means, David?'

'Not really'.

'In this country, unlike in your West, we execute traitors and spies. Only way to safeguard state'.

'Execute!' This is way beyond any joke. When I get out of here, I'll be writing a stern letter to the Tourist Board about all this. If I get out …

'But me', Boris Daniilovich says, patting my hand, 'I don't like the blood-sheddings. I like to give what you say … benefit of doubts. Yes, let us go to find these persons'.

Trouble is, I am by no means certain after all where the apartment is and we drive around for quite a while in one of those black cars with the tinted windows. I am about to abandon all hope when I spot the café where I went with Vitya and first met Seryozha and his gang. I shout out and we stop and get out. It occurs to me to try and make a run for it but I am handcuffed to Mitya and flight is impossible. I am hopeful however that even if we don't find any of the crowd in the café the servers will be able to direct us to the apartment.

There is no sign of anyone I recognise and the servers just shrug when questioned. Then one of the customers, a skinny old woman with button-bright eyes, starts to speak. Boris Daniilovich questions her at length, her hands waving in all directions.

'Yes, this woman remembers you. She doesn't know where your friends live but', pointing, 'says you set off that way'.

We walk down the road in the direction indicated, Boris Daniilovich, Mitya and myself and two other uniformed officers. I see how people shrink back as we pass. Then, suddenly, round a corner, there it is, the old yellow-stuccoed structure. I almost jump for joy. Up we labour to the top floor. Boris Daniilovich waits to get his breath before rapping on the door.

After a while a middle-aged woman I don't recognise answers it. They talk and she shakes her head. With reluctance she moves aside to let us in. I am astonished. There is no sign of the studio, none of Seryozha's paintings, just a regular apartment. An old man nodding off to sleep on a chair in the corner, opens scared eyes at the sight of us. Boris Daniilovich talks to him too.

'There are no artists here. These people have lived here for more than twenty years'.

I've suddenly realised what has happened. I'm in a bad movie starring Sandra Bullock. Or maybe I've just misremembered the building. After all, they all look much the same.

'You know something, David', Boris Daniilovich says sadly, 'I want to believe you, I really do. But is getting more difficult'.

'Why would I make this up?'

He shakes his head. 'How can I know?'

I look wildly around, pointing out the window at other buildings in the complex. 'Maybe that place or that ...'

'I am sorry. This is end of road'.

'What do you mean?'

But he just nods at Mitya and says something and Mitya hauls me off. As they stick me back in the black car, I catch sight of Vitya shuffling along in my jeans. I shout for the car to stop but the driver just drives on. Actually, I'm not even sure it is Vitya but I'm convinced about the jeans.

I am back in the cell. There's some mercy at least in that the light bulb hanging from the ceiling is left on continuously, glowing dimly. Not good enough to read by but then I don't have any books or newspapers. Time passes. I think it must be days. Bread, water and some sort of thin soup come and go. How trim I will be when I get out of here. I try to believe that. And to stop myself from going utterly mad, I force myself to exercise in the cramped space, stretches and push-ups, as much as I am able. I try to remember the words of songs and sing them loudly, usually giving up after the first couple of lines.

More and more often I find myself sinking into black despair. And sometimes it seems I am already dead and in hell. After all, how does the monstrous Svidrigailov describe hell in *Crime and Punishment*? A little room, black and grimy, with spiders in the corner.

Of course, they have to come while I am asleep. I am dragged off my mattress and down the corridor, thrown through a door and find myself in some sort of court. Put in a cage. A stern-looking judge presides, hair like a bunch of steel wool, face like a chip off the Ural mountains. Huge breasts the only indication that this is a woman. Good news or bad? I try to smile at her, trying to muster up my famous charm, at the same time thinking how dreadful I must look, unshaven, unwashed, in filthy clothes.

They haven't bothered with an interpreter and I don't have a clue what is being said except that everyone looks grave. I gather there is some sort of half-hearted defence from a pale and skinny man who never makes eye contact with me. The prosecutor does, though. He stares into my eyes so that I have to look away.

A witness is called. It is Vitya. At last grounds for hope. But then I realise, not from what he is saying because I can't understand it, but from his body language that he is giving evidence against me. As he answers each question, the judge's expression gets grimmer and grimmer.

'Vitya', I yell, trying to reach out to him through the bars. 'Tell them I'm innocent. Please tell the truth'.

The judge speaks angrily. My defence council looks at me at last and puts a warning finger to his lips. Vitya also turns, eyes cold and impersonal. Either they have got to him or he has been working for them all along for some reason. One in four. He bows to the judge and leaves the court.

Next up is my first interrogator. He speaks rapidly and looks at me angrily while the judge makes notes. I expect Boris Daniilovich to appear, and hold out some hope that when he does he will be kinder. But suddenly it seems the business is over. The judge leans forward, squashing those enormous breasts painfully against the edge of the table. She growls something to me in Russian.

'I don't understand'.

My first interrogator addresses some words to her and she nods. Then in impeccable English he starts to speak.

'You have been found guilty'.

'What? Guilty of what?'

'The penalty is death'.

I think I scream. I know I fall down and have to be pulled to my feet again by my guard.

'However', the interrogator continues, 'our glorious Soviet State is full of mercy. If you confess your crimes in public, the sentence will be not so severe'.

'But I can't confess when I haven't done anything'.

'If you persist with this idiocy, we cannot help you'.

'I don't know what I am supposed to confess to'.

The interrogator waves a sheet of paper at me. 'This'. It is covered in writing. 'This will be translated into English and you will read it out in front of the camera'.

'I refuse'.

'Then I am sorry for you'.

'I'm just a tourist on holiday. I demand to speak to my ambassador'.

The interrogator sneers. 'You demand!' He laughed and said something to the judge, who also laughs heartily.

'Let me at least talk to Boris Daniilovich ...'

The smile falls from the interrogator's face and crashes to the floor.

'Boris Daniilovich has been relieved of his duties'.

'What? Why?'

'I think you know'.

'I don't. I don't know anything'.

'This court found him guilty. I am afraid mercy shown to you could not be extended to him as traitor to State. Even though he confessed'.

'What do you mean?'

'The counter-revolutionary Jew B.D. Shteynberg has been purged'.

I can't believe this. 'What do you mean? Purged? He's dead?' I look at him with horror.

'Now you see how it is. So you will read the confession?'

They have let me clean myself up. They have brought some of my clothes from the apartment (I am surprised that my roommate hasn't made off with the lot). Mitya brings me into a studio and indicates that I should sit down behind a desk. I haven't yet seen the list of crimes I am supposed to have committed but I have agreed anyway to read them out. What does it matter any more?

I am handed a sheet, an absurd hodgepodge ranging from espionage, black-marketeering, rape, engaging the services of a prostitute (either one or the other surely, but who's listening?) down to illegally staying in a communal flat, public drunkenness and travelling on trams without paying the fare. 'In conclusion', I read aloud, 'I request the Court to register my statement that I fully and completely admit that I am guilty of all the gravest charges brought against me personally, and that I admit my complete responsibility for the treason and treachery I have committed'.

I finish the accursed thing. What will happen to me now? Back to the cell, off to a labour camp. Or will they execute me anyway, like they did Boris Daniilovich?

The door opens and my nameless interrogator enters. He is smiling like a crocodile.

'Very good, David. Very good. So now you can go'.

'What?'

'Yes, indeed. Our State has decided to show infinite mercy. Pardon comes from the very top'. He taps his nose as if I am supposed to understand.

I can't stand. I am overcome with emotion. He takes my hand, raises me up and leads me to the door. Mitya steps aside to let us pass. A long dark corridor stretches into infinity. My interrogator gestures to me to go. I think of the non-believer Ivan Karamazov who maintained that if he found after death that he could reach paradise if he walked a quadrillion kilometres, he would still refuse to move. But then, after standing firm for another thousand years, in the end he started to walk anyway.

I start to walk away, down the corridor. Now I see that there is a door at the far end. As I go I wonder if, like the hero of Arthur Koestler's *Darkness at Noon*, it will end here with a bullet in the back of the neck. I am almost afraid to glance back, convinced I will see Mitya standing there aiming his gun at me. As long as I don't look back, there is hope. I walk on as steadily as I can, forcing myself not to run. Will I look? Will I? I hear the click of a safety catch being released and know for certain that in one minute, in one second, it will all be over.

But I walk on and approach the door. Will they truly let me go?

I grips the handle and still I hold my breath. I turn the handle and push the door away from me …

Whatever I thought might be on the other side, it was never this. Never this. But perhaps after all I should have known. The end of every tour I've ever been on leads into the souvenir shop. The gauntlet the tourist has to run past, shelf upon shelf of tat. It's the same here. Matrioshka dolls of Soviet leaders from Lenin (very small) to Brezhnev (very big). Tea cloths featuring Soviet slogans. Posters, mugs, t-shirts, pens, key rings, all with Soviet emblems. Fur hats, garishly painted wooden spoons and bowls, amber jewellery, metal trays decorated with folk motifs, tea glasses in tin holders featuring a leaf motif round an embossed neo-classical building.

Someone grips my arm.

This is it, I think. They are tantalising me, only to drag me back into the pit.

But the someone is laughing, bubbles in champagne, and tossing brown curls. Irina.

'You naughty boychik, you run from me'.

I look at her.

'Where have you been?' I say.

'Where have I? Ha! Is good. I come to apartment. You are not there'. She pulls a face. 'They tell me you go out with man. So I know you find new friends. Is good for you but what about poor Irina ... left all alone …'

Poor Irina.

'Well', she continues. 'Never mind it. Chief thing you have the good times'.

I see the exit and start to shuffle towards it, hoping not to call attention to myself too much with inordinate haste. Irina is still pulling at my sleeve.

'So how you like our Soviet World Experience, David? You think you know now how it feels to live in such a system? Yes? Horror show?'

It catches my eye and I pause and pick it up. An icon. It looks just like Auntie's. Only trouble is, there are at least twenty of them, all the same.

'Clever the way they make them look so old', Irina says. 'You want to buy?'

'No', I say. 'Thank you but no thanks'.

Back at my Moscow hotel I find neatly folded on the bed my jeans and shirt with my wallet and papers, even Seryozha's scratchy drawing which I still can't make head nor tail of, my watch and camera. I check the shots. There is no sign of the incriminating photos of blueprints and military installations. The drunk outside the shop is there, and a grinning Vitya and the beggars by the church. I pass them by. But I sit looking for a long while at the one of Lyuba provocatively dressed, standing in front of the KGB headquarters where I was held, as it turns out according to the date on my watch, for just a few hours and not the days I had imagined.

Or have I imagined them? I raise my eyes and see myself faintly reflected in the blank TV screen, a man, gaunt and hollow-eyed, hunched at a table reading out a long confession. And then I blink and the image disappears.

If You Go Out in the Woods Today

'Capital idea', Mr Rooney exclaimed when Kevin asked for time off. 'Capital, dear boy. I was going to suggest the very same thing myself, don't you know'.

Capital, indeed, thought Kevin. Dear boy, indeed. Who used that sort of language anymore? But Mr Rooney – always Mister to his staff and never Neville – was old school through and through, dapper in his Homburg hat (ever at a jaunty tilt), his black suit with the red carnation in the buttonhole, a fresh one daily. A white-haired old gent who nonetheless swam in the sea every day of the year and urged his staff to do likewise.

'Keeps the blood charged up, don't you know'.

Mr Rooney, heart of evil, as the joke went among the staff from his given name, Neville, though it was a bit unfair. Mr Rooney was fine unless you slacked off. Then and only then he showed the sharpness of his teeth.

Now he was exhorting Kevin, 'go away out of the city, dear boy. Get some fresh air into those jaded lungs of yours'.

Bloody cheek. What did Mr Rooney know about his lungs? That was something between Kevin's doctor and himself alone. But he was grateful, too. He had been feeling low for a long time. Troubled in some indefinable way. The thought of long tramps through the crisp winter countryside was irresistible.

'Just the ticket', said Mr Rooney. 'Somewhere up in the mountains. Blow away the cobwebs. What the doctor ordered, don't you know'.

My God, thought Kevin.

The young man seated behind the reception desk smiled up at him. Smiled widely, revealing uneven teeth that were ever so slightly yellow. But perhaps you only noticed them, Kevin thought, because the young man's complexion was so very white, chalky even. Smooth hair the blue-black colour of a magpie's wing. And lips a little too full and rosy.

'Four nights, sir', the young man was saying. 'Is that correct, sir?'

'Yes', Kevin replied. 'And my sister will be arriving the day after tomorrow for a couple of nights'.

'Your sister. Ah'. The young man's small black eyes twinkled as if to say no need for excuses or explanations, none of my business. Kevin decided suddenly that despite that smile he disliked him intensely. Actually he wasn't sure about the hotel either, but it would be too complicated to change arrangements now. No doubt it would do, but the granite edifice, with its draughty and gloomy entrance hall hung with the heads of dead animals, muggy with the perfume of the lilies arranged in large vases as if in a funeral parlour, was depressing to say the least. In his already low state of mind, a bright new building, all glass and pale stone and abstract art, buzzing with life, would have been preferable to this empty mausoleum.

Mr Rooney had suggested it.

'Lovely old place, dear boy. Full of character, don't you know'.

Kevin's room, which he grudgingly had to admit was perfectly adequate – comfortable twin beds, immaculate linen, spotless en suite – looked out over a stretch of boggy green turf and across a stream to a looming wall of mountain that blocked out all sunlight. If there had been any sunlight. It had started raining heavily as he drove the seventy or so kilometres from the city, and still showed no sign of stopping. It was as if a thick grey veil were being drawn across the valley rendering the mountain a ghost of itself. When he opened the window to see better, his net curtain was torn out by the wind, the rain blasting in on him. He could hear the deluge surging, roaring over rocks.

He retrieved the sodden curtain and shut the window and all became quiet and still again. Laying himself down on the satiny counterpane he closed his eyes. By God, he was tired. Perhaps after all there was something physically wrong with him even though his doctor had said not at all. Just overwork, stress. But his doctor was of the laid-back school who favoured painkillers for pain without inquiring into deeper causes.

He must have slept because when he opened his eyes again it was already dusk outside. And still raining hard. His head was splitting. Maybe it was a brain tumour. His doctor hadn't suggested tests. Kevin should have insisted.

Down in the restaurant he ordered the special. An anonymous soup, followed by a sort of stew with lumps of meat submerged in a browny sauce and, for dessert, a spongy pudding speckled with what looked to be the droppings of some small mammal but which were probably raisins. It tasted of nothing at all but Kevin didn't care. He was no gourmet. He wondered what Jess would make of it all the same. Jess liked good food. Maybe there were other, better things on the menu but he was too weary to check.

He had a beer in the bar but there was no atmosphere, no distracting buzz of life. Only a couple of ancient men hunched at opposite ends of the varnished wooden counter. The young receptionist was serving and smiled across at him constantly as if encouraging conversation. But Kevin couldn't be bothered. Whatever could they have to say to each other? He finished his drink quickly and, although it was only nine o'clock, decided to go up to bed.

There didn't seem to be any one else staying in the place, yet for some reason he had been allocated a room at the end of a long corridor. He'd only had the one beer but already felt woozy and staggered slightly. Another sure sign, he reckoned, that all was not well health-wise. He made a note to inform his doctor that he was suffering from vertigo on top of everything else. To help his balance he fixed his eyes on the floor, on the carpet and noticed for the first time the design on its muddy-hued background, lozenges of colour that, as he looked more closely, seemed to take on the form of an army of giant beetles with red backs, green legs and bulging yellow eyes, antennae a-quiver. They marched the length of the corridor and, when he opened his door, on into his room. And now that the distasteful notion had lodged in his head he couldn't get rid of it. He walked in gingerly fashion over the carpet as if to avoid crushing the creatures.

This place really was a mistake. Despite the difficulty getting a signal, he would try and phone Jess the next morning and tell her not to come. Or to find them another hotel. He opened his window a tiny crack, for fresh air, climbed into bed and fell into a heavy sleep to the roar of the headlong stream.

As usual for him, he woke in the early hours, in darkness. His watch indicated 4.47. The familiar panic had set in, a sickness in his stomach that turned his bowels liquid. Stress, right, but weren't most serious illnesses caused by stress? Who was to say, without tests, that it wasn't colon cancer? His doctor had prescribed sleeping pills but you'd be mad to take them so near to dawn. He rolled over in bed knowing he wouldn't get any more rest that night.

The morning light cracked through the curtains and across his face like a whip. Kevin opened sticky eyes. With a shudder he saw that the bugs were now crawling from the floor up the curtains, their bodies gleaming, their antennae alert. Maybe crawling up over him too. He leapt out of bed. Then realised the apparent march of the bugs was just the effect of the breeze agitating the pattern on the fabric. He even managed a weak chuckle at his fancies, no doubt the residue of some dream he could no longer remember. But there was light, and somewhere the sun was shining, and, as he craned out of his window he saw that the sky over the mountain was blue. Shaving, he even found himself humming. He had after all slept through to a reasonable time. Things were looking up as so often on a new day. No need after all to warn off Jess. She'd laugh at him anyway as she always did.

He was planning a long ramble and so had decided to fortify himself with the full cooked breakfast. Even the sickening residue of grease in his mouth couldn't dispel his euphoria, though there was again surprisingly little taste to the sausages and rashers, the black and white pudding, the fried eggs. He ate it all anyway, washed down with tarry tea.

The young man took his key with a big yellow smile.

'Do you want a map, sir?' he asked, seeing that Kevin was geared up for a walk, sports jacket and sturdy shoes.

'No need, the path is way marked', Kevin said. 'Impossible to get lost'.

The young man's eyes twinkled. 'Ah … But still …' He waved the map at him. 'Just in case?'

'No, really'.

'Well then, if you're sure. Just don't blame me ...' The young man laughed merrily. 'And I hope you haven't forgotten your rain gear'.

Kevin snorted. Was the idiot joking? There wasn't a cloud in the sky. He wasn't about to weigh himself down with a load of unnecessary stuff, even abandoning his phone. He turned to leave.

'Well, have a nice day then, sir'.

The insincerity of the remark didn't warrant a reply and Kevin just grunted and left.

The path along the stream led eventually to a lake, as he ascertained from the information board at the start of the walk. You could hike its length and then, if you so wished, you could take a zig-zag track up the mountainside and make a great loop back, eventually descending near the hotel again. There was history here as well, a monastic site built over a pre-Christian settlement. The ruins were said to be picturesque.

For a while the path ran between stream and mountain. Strewn down the steep slope, among shrubs and evergreens, were rocks and boulders, tumbled ages ago, moss and lichen-covered. On the other side, between path and rain-bloated stream, lay open ground punctuated with just an occasional tree. Most of them birches, though birches stripped, presumably by harsh weather, of their top coat of bark, so that they glowed pink rather than silver. Disconcertingly for Kevin, it struck him that it was exactly the colour of flesh, specifically of Sarah's flesh, and where two thin trees curled around each other, the effect was almost obscene, like thighs entwined.

A large boulder with a deep horizontal split across its face seemed to smile lasciviously back at him.

'What are you grinning at?' Kevin said aloud. Then looked round embarrassed in case anyone had heard him. But there was no one else. No one at all.

His mood had been good up to now but thoughts of Sarah were definitely unwelcome and he tried to banish them. Every so often, however, another stripped tree would remind him. This one, for instance, its bark split into two legs over exposed inner tissue, unpleasantly reminded him of their final meeting, she lying back naked on the bed, legs apart, careless of his gaze, her face turned away, her body unresponsive. Like he wasn't there. Like she was already dead.

Soon the path moved deeper into woods, the sheerness of the mountainside overhung with ferns and creepers that here and there masked the darker mouths of caves. Runnels of water from springs augmented by the previous day's rain crashed down between rocks and into gulleys. On the other side of the path, a forest of slender birches wading in marsh were thankfully no longer agitatingly nude but become mossy as though subject to verdigris. A soft greenness covered all. It was restful and Kevin calmed down again.

Then the path opened out and he was confronted with the ancient ruins of the monastic settlement. It was a millennium since monks had worked and worshipped here. Much longer since the saint had founded it. A time when this valley would have been remote and almost inaccessible. And yet older signs were here too, of much older inhabitants, a standing stone circle, a dolmen, a ring fort, the site of pagan worship and ritual. Sacrifice. Homage to old gods.

Kevin lingered in a roofless church, one of several at the site. On the grass around it lurched stone slabs, worn with age, the graves of monks, some rectangular, some crudely cruciform, with one high cross from a later time, on which a weathered knot pattern could still faintly be discerned. Kevin didn't consider himself superstitious and yet the place gave him the creeps. He walked on.

Now the path led round the accessible side of the lake, its waters sparkling in the sunlight. He strode easily along beneath pines and lacy winter-bleached larches. Again his mood lifted. The cobwebs were definitely blowing away.

He had omitted to bring anything to drink with him but no matter. At every moment more springs gushed down the slopes. His hands made cups for water so icy it prickled his mouth.

Eventually the path emerged out of the woods at the extreme end of the lake, where boulders larger than any yet had, aeons before, tumbled into massy piles. A miners' village had been built here, long-deserted, of granite houses, unroofed now and inundated so that ponds filled the rooms where people had once lived. Kevin had to pick his way over slippery stepping stones to reach dry land again.

He sat to rest on a boulder, munching on a chocolate bar. Such stillness. But listen! Could he hear faint voices, were those figures flitting through the buildings? Not at all. It was just the wind and the play of shadow on stone. There was nothing here now, only absence. Then some movement caught his eye and high above he could see feral goats prancing on the very edge of the precipice. How could they be up there and not fall? Beyond them, at the end of the valley, he could make out his own safer path zigzagging up beside a thundering waterfall. He took a breath and started the climb.

His heart pounded painfully on the way and he had to stop frequently to let it wind down and to catch his breath. (More worrying symptoms to keep an eye on). However he was determined to press onwards and upwards, he'd be glad of it in the end, he knew. But by the time Kevin got to the head of the waterfall, he sensed a chill in the air not just from the altitude, which despite all his huffing and puffing wasn't so very great. Clouds had drifted in over the blue, and the breeze was rising. He stood for a moment looking back over the lake, still picturesque although dangerous too: no longer masked by sunlight, its inky pit revealing how the mountainside must continue plunging steeply under its surface, who knew how far down. The surrounding lower slopes were skirted with thick woodland but the treeline gave way nearer the summit to open heath, save in one place where a descending line of wind-warped trees, silhouetted against the sky, resembled, to his eye, nothing less than a herd of wild horses, manes tossed, frozen in their gallop down the precipitous cliff face. Beyond the lake, far in the distance, he could discern the walls of the monastic city, the dolmen, the stone circle, rock on rock.

A sudden sharper gust hit him sideways and Kevin all but toppled over. The clouds were clotting together, blacker now and he shivered, sensing the imminence of rain. He felt aggrieved. The earlier blue sky and sunshine had tricked him into leaving his waterproof jacket behind. Perhaps it would be wiser to turn back. But he hated that. Having to concede failure. To confront the I-told-you-so expression on the receptionist's nasty little face. And after all, how far could it be, now that he had almost reached the highest point of his walk? No, he would press on. What harm a little rain? Time anyway to get moving. A post with a yellow arrow on it told him which way to go, since now there was no longer a clearly-defined path. By keeping to the ridge he would be going in the right direction, surely, until he came to the next way mark.

And so it was, tramping up over open heath, checking for yellow arrows, looking down at the lake and the low path he had so recently been walking. His legs had initially felt sluggish after the steep climb but now, his energy renewed, Kevin was exhilarated, so far from anyone and anywhere, far from the dreary grind of work and Mr Rooney. Far from thoughts, more to the point, of Sarah, all that sorry business like a dream now. And surely it was a dream. It had to be. Up here it was as if he had shed all that baggage. Heart and breathing fine now, just a question of adjusting and he felt fitter than for a long time. Top of the world, Mr Rooney, just the ticket. No jaded lungs here. He strode on, the arrows still pointing upwards, however, rising much higher than he had thought. But that was fine, too. He even whistled.

So when did Kevin come to realise that he was lost? Not for an hour at least. Only when it occurred to him that he hadn't seen a way mark for a long while. When clouds ambushed him, wrapping themselves tightly around him, pressing down over him like a damp blanket, like a terrible memory, and he was unable to see the lake or the ridge or anything around himself, hardly able to breath. Stumbling over rocks and roots, he felt sick to his soul. Was this then her revenge, his retribution? But he wasn't superstitious. He didn't believe any of that rubbish. No, it was absurd to panic. All he had to do was turn left and he would reach the ridge again soon enough. He turned and was relieved to find, after a while, some sort of a path again. And paths always lead somewhere, don't they? He followed it for a while, its plunging descent, until trees loomed around him. Could this be right? He tried to remember the map he had seen on the information board. Was there a wood?

Now branches reached out of the mist, twisted and deformed. Far worse, the path had disappeared into mud, only marked with the occasional cloven hoof print, and he started to fear that he had simply been following a goat trail. Could he go back? He tried but couldn't find his own tracks and now didn't even know which direction was which. But down had to be good, surely. Down and down, steeper and steeper, clambering, holding on to the beckoning branches so as not to slip, until suddenly he emerged, yes, but on a precipice that dropped into darkness.

Darkness? He checked his watch. Surely it couldn't be evening already. His watch said not but the light was going. No doubt about it. And him up here with not a notion of where he was and no phone and no one but the young man at the hotel even aware that he had gone for a walk. Somewhere, could be anywhere.

He attempted to skirt around the precipice. No good. The overhang was too perilous. He would have to go back after all. If only he knew where back was? He took some deep breaths. Still no need to panic. After all, what was the worst thing that could happen? The worst? To die of exposure here on the cold mountain. He let out a little cry. But no, he wouldn't let that happen. If he had to spend the night up here – and that was by no means certain, there were hours to go yet – the main thing would be to keep warm (he was shivering, but more with dread than cold). And the mist would surely have lifted by morning.

Before that, for as long as there was any light left, he would try, he would try, to get down. At last he found another way that looked more promising, no great obstacles, he was out of the thicket now and still descending. How, he thought to himself, he and Jess would laugh together at his adventure, sitting by a fire, hot drinks in hand. And food. Yes, food would be good. For he was hungry, having eaten the one and only chocolate bar he had brought with him much earlier when he stopped in the deserted village. Hungry and thirsty too, but there was no sound of rushing water here. Or was there? Kevin strained his ears. Yes, yes, there was. Distant but definite. He worked his way towards the thudding sound. And then the wind ...

He was running now, tripping, trying to get away. The horses were almost upon him, he could feel the heat of their snorting breath. For it wasn't a fall of water he had heard but the pounding of hooves galloping down the mountainside. He mustn't pause to think how could this be? He was running for his life, and the wild horses, tossing their manes, were right behind him.

He fell, tumbling over rocks, clutching desperately at hummocks of grass that came away in his hands, trying to stop the momentum but still to get away. Now he was in a ditch and the horses leaping over him. He saw their panicked red eyes as they passed. Not chasing, then, but fleeing. Whatever it was, he must get away too. But he was so very thirsty.

Water was trickling into the ditch and he gulped it down again, that same icy, slightly metallic taste biting at his teeth. And something else. Some tang. Blood. The water was brown with blood …

The wind howled, tossing shreds of mist around him, battering the mountainside. Tore at Kevin where he sat shaking uncontrollably in the partial shelter of a rock, attempting to gather his thoughts. To calm himself. He was wet and bruised but whole, no bones were broken, no ankles sprained. And of course there were no horses. His imagination had twisted them into being out of cloud, wind and shadows. There was no blood, just water brown with peat from the bog. How absurd to fancy anything else. He was in a bad situation, yes, but not a hopeless one. Not yet.

He cautiously continued his descent.

And oh joy! At last he was pulling himself out of the web of mist. And despite the gathering gloom, he could still just about find his way down, down.

It was the lake, black as oil. He almost tumbled in, so steep it was here. And the rocks kept plunging down: there was no strand for him to walk on. Perhaps he could wade. He leaned over and tested the depths with a stick but could feel no bottom to it. The rain was sheeting down now, lashing him, making the rocks even more treacherous and slippery. But there was no alternative: he must make his way round the cliff side, clinging to it as to a frigid lover. At every moment he feared tumbling into freezing waters.

Suddenly he came upon a cave. Kevin climbed in and found welcome respite, enfolding himself in its musky darkness. Perhaps this was the very cave to which the saintly hermit had retreated all those centuries before. Was it from here he beat off the woman devil who had come naked to tempt him from his prayers? Beating her with nettles so that she fell into the lake and drowned. Kevin rested for a while in the cave thinking about that woman, thinking that if she drowned she was no devil. A temptress, yes, but a woman of flesh. The saint had justified murder by demonising her and no one judged him. Saints could get away with things like that.

Unbidden thoughts of Sarah returned. How she hadn't understood his need. How she had stubbornly refused to understand. What had happened was her fault entirely. Now she lay before him again, legs, torso bare as the twisted trunks of stripped birches. Her face turned away. Her long hair tangled with water weeds. He could feel the pulse beating in her neck. Sink into her darkness. Her corpse-like stillness.

No, he mustn't think of Sarah any more. Ever again. He must move on. Get out of here. Save himself.

God alone knew where he had ended up. In some sort of marsh at the edge of the lake. He had to cross it in order to be free, but with each step he sank into waterlogged ground that pulled at him. Each step had to be dragged out again, with each step he seemed to be sinking deeper. Night had fallen now, but the storm had passed and an occasional star pricked the sky. He trudged on, cold, wet, and yes, frightened. Darker shapes loomed out of darkness. This place was evil, hungry. He knew that now for sure. Skeletal fingers were touching him, clutching at him, tearing at him, long hair brushing his face, creepers and low branches hanging from the rock face over the marsh. He sank up to his thigh in mud and cried out. To extricate himself he had to grasp one of those vicious arms, blood running from his hands where thorns punctured the skin. The marsh kept his shoe, a trophy.

'Oh, you want them, do you?' Kevin shouted. 'All right, so. I'll give you the other?' He yanked off his remaining shoe, flinging it away. He pulled off his sodden socks, too. The bog felt glutinous under his bare feet, caressing between his toes. Wanting him. No. No.

He stumbled out. There were sharp stones underfoot now, slashing at the flesh. But he didn't care. He was out. Nearly out. On he went. On and on.

Ahead of him tall shapes. Shapes like men. Fearfully he approached them (he could go no other way). Then he recognised the standing stones. Nearly wept with joy. They watched him but he didn't care. Nearly out.

Soft grass under his feet. Soothing.

But he had to cross the graveyard, where the lurching tombstones were even now resolving into monks, their blank faces turning towards him.

And there – my God – taller than any, on a hummock above him, framed against the sky, why, it was Mr Rooney of all people. Neville himself. Heart of evil. Homburg and all.

'Dear boy', he said. 'My dear, dear boy, whatever have you been up to?'

'Why did you send me here, Mr Rooney?' Kevin's voice cracked.

Mr Rooney laughed. 'Don't you know by now, dear boy? Don't you know?'

But of course, it wasn't Mr Rooney at all. The high cross with its stone ring stood dark against the night sky. That's all it was. All it ever was.

Until it moved. Until it started to move towards him. And all around, the monks or whatever they were, began pulling themselves out of the ground and started crowding towards him too.

He screamed and Mr Rooney laughed and then Kevin ran. Exhausted as he was he ran. Not looking back. Ran back along what was surely the path to the hotel, light, people, civilisation. Ran and ran and ran in his bare feet, aware of the steadily pursuing throng, monks and those from the dark ages before, sliding after him, gaining on him. Kevin ran but seemed to make no progress, some force was pulling him back. And then they reached him and pushed and trampled him into the marshy ground. He tried to pull himself up but the marsh was pulling him in, and Mr Rooney was laughing, and all the monks were laughing and Sarah spread her fleshy legs wide and laughed too and the boulder grinned its wide grin at him, grasses tumbling out of its hungry gob. And Kevin rolled himself into a ball, hands over his head, and knew it was all just a mad fancy and that he would open his eyes in a minute and there would be nothing there except for himself and the path and the wood and he would get up and go home. Home. He opened his eyes and yes, he was right, there was nothing there, no Mr Rooney, no monks. No Sarah, thank God. But still he couldn't get up. Try as he might to get a grip on the earth, it slid away beneath his fingers and he felt a cold chill rising up under him, into him, through him. He couldn't move at all. Not a muscle.

'Your brother, ah yes', the smiling young man was saying to the pretty woman facing him across the reception desk. 'Yes, indeed. Well, he went for a walk'.

Jess smiled back. She was inclined to be friendly, even though first impressions hadn't been favourable. What an old-fashioned hotel. Those moth-eaten animal heads. That heavy scent. And what, despite or perhaps because of that smile, an unnerving young man. He looked unhealthy. There was definitely a greenish tinge to that pale complexion. The unnaturally-black hair. The pinhead eyes. The rose-pink on his lips seeming artificial. Surely it couldn't be lipstick.

'Do you happen to know where he was going?' she asked.

'Alas', the young man replied. 'He never said. Although most people take the green lane along the stream to the monastic city. He may have gone that way'.

Jess didn't feel like waiting around for Kevin in this creepy place, eyed up by that creepy young man. 'Thank you', she said. 'I'll try that'.

And taking the proffered map, she set off.

'A nice polite young lady', the young man said to the stuffed elk head hanging over the entrance. 'Not like her rude brother. And so very pretty. But oh dearie me', he giggled. 'What a scatterbrain I am. I clean forgot to tell her that it wasn't today her brother went out for his walk. Not today. It was yesterday. Oh dear'. And he laughed again that shrill little laugh.

Mr Rooney couldn't have been kinder. He was the only person Jess could think of to contact when Kevin failed to turn up after two days. Mr Rooney immediately drove down from the city to help with the search.

'Goodness', he'd exclaimed when they first met, 'Never in my wildest dreams, don't you know, would I ever have suspected that our dear Kevin had such a lovely sister'.

Jess had tried to smile at the compliment.

'But I feel so guilty, dear girl', he went on. 'I was worried about him, do you see. I thought the country air would do him good'.

'No need to feel bad. It was a kind thought'.

'But it was me, do you see, who suggested this particular place. I used to come here many years ago'. He looked around as if pleasantly reminiscing. Perhaps he could see attractions that she had missed. 'Ah yes ...'

All the same, Jess was taken with him, his old-fashioned mannerly ways, his elegance, the jauntily angled Homburg hat, the silk scarf, the red carnation in his buttonhole. An avuncular presence. She felt reassured. If anyone could help, Mr Rooney was surely that man.

'Let's go out again, my dear. Dreadful to sit here doing nothing. Maybe we can find some clue to indicate what's happened'.

'I've been out there so many times, Mr Rooney'.

'Neville, my dear. Please call me Neville. You will won't you'. Smiling so kindly.

She nodded.

'Now, my dear', he went on in that reassuring way of his, 'it must have happened to me a million times, looking everywhere for something I've misplaced. I can't believe it hasn't happened to you too'. He paused, pale eyes twinkling, a skinny finger raised. 'You search and you search and then, lo and behold, it turns up in the very first place you looked, don't you know'.

Was he really comparing the loss of Kevin to spectacles or keys or an unpaid bill?

Then he laughed and patted her hand, and took hold of it. His felt papery. Only being kind, trying to make light of things. That was it, bless him. Him and his old-fashioned ways. But though old, she thought, he was still handsome and clearly fit. He had told her he swam every day in the sea. They walked to the lake and started back.

'I knew it', Jess said. 'I knew there'd be nothing'.

Well, there had been a shoe. But that could have been anyone's.

'Hardly a glass slipper', Mr Rooney had quipped.

She found the remark insensitive but then realised that Mr Rooney, in his kindness, was again just trying to cheer her up.

'My dear girl', he now said, offering her a handkerchief to cry into. It was a big white linen square, embroidered with the initials NR, and smelt freshly laundered. And something else. The scent of lilies. 'Why not sit down for a moment, dear girl', he continued. 'Here on this rock. The one that looks like a big smiley face'.

He even spread his silk scarf on the boulder so the seat of her dress wouldn't get stained with lichen. He sat beside her, close.

'You know, dear girl', Mr Rooney said softly, taking her hand again and pressing it. 'I hate to say this but I think you should prepare yourself'.

She lifted big tearful eyes to his.

'Kevin was at a very low ebb this last while, don't you know. He was troubled. I think it was something to do with a girl. A dear, dear girl who used to work for us too. Then she left. Suddenly. Not a word to anyone. Dropped off the face of the earth. Did you know about that? About Sarah?'

Jess shook her head. 'We haven't met up much recently. He never talked about personal matters'.

'No', said Mr Rooney. 'I don't suppose he did. A bottler-upper, that was our dear Kevin'.

'Was?' asked Jess fearfully. 'You think he's had some sort of terrible accident? I know it's been a couple of days but he could be up in the mountains, couldn't he, with a broken ankle or something. No phone'.

'Yes, that was foolish to say the least. Leaving his phone behind. And Arnold, the dear, dear boy at reception, says Kevin just waved away the maps that Arnold wanted to give him. Arnold, you see, warned him, dear girl. But he just wouldn't listen'.

Mr Rooney lifted her chin and held it so that her face was close to his. She could smell his pepperminty breath, see the broken veins on his nose and cheeks. 'The search party will find him if he can be found. The helicopter. But you know ...'

'What? What is it?'

'I think he may have decided ... dear girl ...' Now he put his arms around her shoulder and eased her to him. 'The lake is deep. He wouldn't be the first'.

She choked with sobs and put her head against his breast. He pulled her tighter, crushing her cheek against the red carnation.

Kevin was watching them. He had observed Jess every time she walked past. Now he saw them rise to leave. Jess and Mr Rooney, his arm still tightly around her. Mr Rooney picking up his silk scarf and sniffing it, sniffing it. The two of them beginning to move away, Mr Rooney whispering into her ear and just for a second, turning his head to look back. Was that a sly smile? Was that a wink? Did his lips mouth something? Dear boy?

'No! Don't trust him, Jess. His heart is evil. Look at me, Jess. I'm here beside you. Can't you recognise me? Help me. Help me'.

Kevin tried to cry out, as he had before whenever she passed. But he couldn't move his jaw. Couldn't move anything. Calcified as he was. Turned to a lump of stone as he was. The plain fact being that Kevin wouldn't move anything ever again. Eyes fixed open, fixed forever on the naked flesh of a stripped birch tree.

Time passed. Moss growing on him. Lichen. Grasses sprouting out of the rictus of his mouth. And an army of tiny bugs marching over him, shiny red backs, green legs, bulging yellow eyes, antennae a-quiver.

The Woman who Lost a Man on the Train

The title says it all. Or, to be more precise, says it all but also leaves many questions unanswered. The woman lost a man. No doubt about it. The evidence is there. But the who, the why, the where, if that's relevant, remain so far unclear. So are there any answers to these questions? Are there, in cod philosophy, ever any answers?

What is known is that the woman and the man got on the train together at some point. Maybe at the terminus? The man was seen to stow a small blue pull-along case on the rack above the seats. Then they sat across from each other, a table in between. She was positioned facing the engine, while he looked back in the direction from which they had come. Does this matter? Is it significant?

He was a rough-looking individual in his forties, with a shaved head, short and stocky, wearing a grubby white shell jacket with a hood, grey tracksuit bottoms and muddy white trainers. When he removed his jacket, blue tattoos were revealed on his arms, blurry old designs, a rose, a snake, an illegible name.

For her part, she was a big woman with small eyes and a small mouth, hair pulled so tightly back into a doughnut that it looked as if her scalp had been varnished light brown. She wore little make-up on a face which was beginning to sag into middle-age, but her eyebrows were plucked into surprised arcs and her long nails were carefully manicured and painted pearly pink. She too wore a tracksuit, in shiny pale blue. When she took off the jacket she was seen to be wearing a tight-fitting and low-cut short-sleeved beige top, which clearly revealed the contours of her brassiere where it cut into her flesh. She too had a tattoo on her arm, a line of small hearts outlined in blue and with red centres that stretched from the inside of her right wrist a small way up her forearm.

They spoke not a word to each other, in the way of couples who have said it all already. She drew several magazines out of a plastic bag, luridly-headlined magazines of the sort that thrive on celebrity gossip and photographs that reveal the rich and famous off-guard in unflattering moments. He had a tabloid newspaper which he thumbed through idly. Not pausing at the topless girl, making straight for the sport. But even that didn't distract him for long and he stared out of the window at his rapidly-disappearing past but without any evidence of interest.

Maybe he mumbled something to her when he got up and lurched off towards the back of the train? Maybe he told her he was going to the lavatory or to get a drink? If he did, it was said so quietly that no one else could have heard. She looked up briefly as he left and then resumed her reading.

Time passed and she finished one magazine and picked up the next. She turned her head to look briefly in the direction in which he had gone, then back to the magazine. Could she have said if the train stopped at any point? It was an express, but there were a few scheduled stations on the way.

More time passed. A young dark-skinned man with a trolley passed through the carriage offering hot drinks, soft drinks, snacks. The woman bought a coffee and a small packet of chocolate biscuits, wiping the foam from her lips with a paper napkin and eating the biscuits delicately, licking the tips of her fingers afterwards.

An inspector came to check her ticket. He didn't ask and she didn't mention her companion. Perhaps he had taken his ticket with him? But after the inspector had passed on, she craned her neck round again to look down the train. Next she picked up her mobile phone and punched something into it, then laid it back on the table, glancing at it from time to time as if to check if a message had come in, even though the thing had made no sound.

She finished the second magazine and picked up a third. But her heart may not have been in it at this stage because she didn't even bother to open it. Instead she studied her nails and buffed them with her thumbs as if they weren't already sufficiently pearly. Then she stared out the train window at wet fields (it had started to rain some time before), where black and white cows huddled in a corner, or her eyes glided along a canal bank where a man walked a dog and then along a road which ran briefly beside the railway line, an occasional car on it, a container, a tractor, or she looked as houses started to cluster and thicken, indicating a town that they soon sped through too fast to read the name on the signboard. At one point the train crossed a mighty river and she blinked at the great steel girders that held the bridge in suspension over dark water.

The next time she picked up the mobile it was to punch in a number. She held the phone to her ear but it seemed that no one answered. She clicked the thing off without leaving a message.

She stood up and at that point noticed the jacket on the seat opposite her. He had left it behind. She moved round the table and picked it up, looking uncertain. She looked down the train. Then put the garment back on the seat. Did she think he must at least come back eventually, if only for his jacket? She stood for a while as if indecisive, then sat down again. Perhaps she would have gone looking for him were it not for their belongings, the blue case in the rack in particular. Or maybe she thought that if she left and he came back to find her gone he would be angry or upset.

She stared out the window. The train was now thundering through more fields but the rain had been left behind and a weak winter sun had come out of a clotted sky. Time passed.

Suddenly an announcement was made over the loudspeaker. She jumped as though woken from a trance. They were reaching their final destination. She looked back along the train one last time but now people were blocking the view, standing to collect their belongings and put on their coats. She reached up for the case, her big breasts lifting with the movement. It was heavy and she staggered a little bringing it down. She put on her jacket, then picked up the man's.

The train had stopped and people were getting off. She moved along the queue and stepped down from the train, casting a searching eye both ways along the platform. Then she moved to the exit, pulling the case behind her, the man's jacket over her arm, and she disappeared into the crowd and into the night.

Or maybe that's not quite how it happened. Rewind a little ...

She was looking at the man's grubby white jacket lying on the seat. Maybe after all she left it where it was and got off without it.

Or maybe, as she reached to get down her case, her big breasts lifting with the effort, a man across the aisle who had been watching her all through the journey, noting her every move and gesture, now jumped up and offered to help her. She looked at him for the first time and her thin lips twisted in a smile that might have seemed to accentuate her misery. A smile that aborted any intended invitation.

Or maybe the man came back after all. But in that case there would be no story and the title would be a lie. Better perhaps if a man came back and sat down, without speaking and she looked at him and he looked at her. It wasn't the first man, however, but a different one, with different tattoos on his arms, spelling a different message. But when the time came to get off the train, he stood up and put on the man's jacket that had been left on the seat and lifted down the case. And she eased her heavy body out of the seat and shuffled down the crowded aisle behind him, stepping off the train and walking along the platform, pulling the case, him striding ahead but looking back from time to time to make sure she was still there, the two of them disappearing together into the crowd and into the night.

Cliff Edge

'Holy Christ', Fats is yelling, thumping his hands on the steering wheel. 'Holy fucking Christ'.

I'm as high as he is but careful not to show it.

'Watch the road', I say.

'Jesus, Quentin. Jesus!'

'Ok, ok', I manage to laugh. 'Enough of the blaspheming'.

'Wha'?'

He's a pig after all, of the snuffling, truffling sort.

'Curse words, Fats'.

'Yeah but ... fuck …'

And he laughs too, like he's got phlegm in his throat and can't shift it. Then suddenly he jams on the brakes, stops the car, jumps out and vomits into the long grass. I look at his bent-over pig's body, his arse half out of his jeans. I want to shove him too, into whatever garbage he has puked up. But I grip the seat and stay put. My heart is pounding, my head is fizzing. I did it.

'Jesus, Quentin', Fats is saying as he gets back in the car. 'I can't believe what you just fucking did'.

'Yeah well ...' I'm cool. 'So what'.

We'd been out on the cliff path, two guys taking exercise the way they always say you should, to keep healthy and that. There'd been this party in one of them big fancy houses way up on the hill with gardens that run down to the cliff edge. Not our scene really but, see, after those wankers who decide these things decided Fats wasn't entitled any longer to a job-seeker's allowance on account of he wasn't seeking a job, he'd been forced to move into the supply business. And the only reason rich dude had us there at his fucking do in the first place was for Fats to bring in the goods and keep the guests happy with a selection box of MDMA, ketamine and pills, to background music from fucking Sigur Ros or Mulatu Astartqe (I like to check out the CDs on these occasions). Stuck-up freaks the lot of them, specially the heifers with the implants Daddy had paid for, the all-over tans not from a bottle but from sunbathing nudy at their villas in the Med, their designer rags, their silly tight little mouths that only ate rich cock.

They never stopped going all fucking night and then just passed out, like someone suddenly turned the lights off. Fats and me were too jizzed up to sleep and in any case our work there was done, so we left with the dawn, climbing over the bodies, wrapped round each other, out of it, like the morning after some fucking Roman orgy you'd see in the movies. My idea to take a walk, suss out the possibilities. I mean, these houses have massive security gates at the front but I wanted to see if you could just hop over some rickety back gate or plough through bushes on the cliff side. Make some mental notes, like. Never know when the knowledge would come in handy.

Fats was whinging on, of course. Puffing and blowing like a beached fucking whale, and taking blasts of his inhaler every few seconds. Fats isn't a walker under any circumstances but I promised we'd circle back to the car after a bit. So anyway, to console himself, Fats started popping what was left of his store, washed down with a bottle of vodka he'd found lying about, mixed three to one with Coke from a litre bottle he was carrying in a Tesco bag. Classy that way, Fats is. He offered me some but I didn't need that stuff, not the pills, not the booze. Not me. Self control and abstinence, that's my kick.

'Taste that air', I said, just to annoy him, filling my lungs at the same time, striding ahead. 'Fucking invigorating', I said.

Fats muttered something and took another puff.

We'd seen the guy from far off.

'What the fuck's he doing?' Fats said.

The guy was on the edge of the cliff, staring out to sea.

'Maybe he's gonna jump', I said.

'You think, you think?' Fats was excited. 'Let's wait and watch'. Even got out his smart phone to take a pic.

'Or maybe he's a twitcher', I said.

'What?'

'Not like you, Fats. Not like you twitch'. He did and all. Especially coming down. Ugly sight. Another reason why I don't do much. 'Bird watcher'.

Yeah, that was it. I could see now the guy had this fancy camera and was pointing it down the cliff side where the gulls or whatever were screaming in that way they had. Up with the lark, to see the fucking birds. What a life.

The path curved round a bit of an inlet, bringing us ever closer to the guy. He had on this stupid striped woolly hat his ould wan had probably knitted for him. Skinny, in a red zip-up jacket and jeans. We got closer. Pink skin, raw from shaving, scraps of grey hair from under the hat. He didn't look our way. We weren't there.

Don't know why. I hadn't planned it. The thought, like they say, hadn't even crossed my mind. I was, to tell the truth, thinking of anything else. The rich kids, their faces smiling pill-stupid, laughing with those orthodontically-perfect fucking teeth you'd like to punch down their throats, sniggering at Fats behind his porcine back (hey, it's only me allowed do that). That fake-blonde heifer with her too-perfect tits out (look what money can buy), dancing to the music, asking the rich dude in her posh accent, loud, 'Who's the spa?' Meaning me. And him whinnying like a fucking horse and saying, 'Oh, that's just another skanger, the help's help'. And she said, 'Help!' And stuck her tits out at me. So when we drew level with the guy on the cliff, I just kind of shoved him over the edge, his screams mingling crazily with the cries of the gulls.

Fats stopped stone still but I didn't even break my stride. Just walked on like a guy out for a morning stroll with his mate. Just like that. Didn't even look to see. Afterwards thought I should have asked the guy first what the birds were. Gulls, yeah, but what sort? Should have asked. See, I'm curious that way, self-improving, like.

Talk about twitching. Fats can't fucking stop. If I could drive, I'd take the wheel. But I've always considered myself the one driven, the one who has others drive for them. Even refer to Fats as 'my personal chauffeur', only half-joking.

'Cool it', I say. 'Cool it'.

'Holy fucking Jesus Christ, Quentin. S'posing someone saw'.

'Who? You?'

'Not me', he says. 'I didn't see nothing'.

'You mean you saw something'.

'What?'

But I'm not inclined to explain the double negative. Not right now.

The car swerves.

'Get a grip Fats. If the cops stop us ...'

'Shit'. He screeches to the kerbside.

'If the cops stop us they'll do you for driving under the influence', I explain. 'Which you and I both would find inconvenient'.

'And the guy ...'

'Na ... nothing to worry about there so long as you keep your fucking lip buttoned'. I glance sideways at him. Fucking loose cannon. But I keep my voice cool. 'The guy slipped in his excitement at seeing all them ... gulls'. Fuck, I'd have to check out them birds. 'Got it, man?'

'Ok. Yeah. Right'.

He manages to drive on relatively ok. Drops me at me ma's. Well, where I live for now.

'Keep cool, man'.

'Yeah, Quentin, right. See yer later'.

'Alligator'.

Fats winces, so I'm thinking maybe I look like one meself. Dangerous. Quentin the Cayman. Yeah.

Ma hears me come in – ears tuned like a fucking bat's – and clumps downstairs in her baby blue dressing gown.

'Ok, Quentin, pet?' she says, hoping as ever I'll give her a loving hug.

'Yeah', I say.

'Good party?' Then when I don't reply. 'Must have been if you're only home now'. Checking her watch. I mean who wears a fucking watch in bed? Only me ma.

'Yeah'.

'Was that Richard dropped you off?'

Richard is Fats.

'Yeah'. Wait for it.

'Had he been drinking?'

'Ah well, you know. Early on, like. Sober enough now'.

'You know I don't think ... I wish you wouldn't ... Quentin, I've said it before, he's a bad influence …'

'Na. Fats ... Richard is sound'.

'Keeping you out till all hours. Just cause you can't drive. I'd have given you the money for a taxi ... Quentin'.

'Yeah'.

She fills the kettle

'Want a cuppa tea?'

And sit here listening to you rabbiting on. No thanks.

'Na, think I'll turn in'.

I can feel her eyes on my back.

'Thanks anyway, ma', I say, throwing her a crumb.

Can't sleep of course. Still fizzing. I did it. I fucking did it. And if Fats yacks, so what. His against mine. And him a well-known crackhead from a what them social worker pricks like to call a dysfunctional family (both parents alcos, both done time, usual thing, stand to reason), while me only child of a respectable widow woman, honours student without a blemish on me ... Just a shame I can't hold down a job. But in this day and age ... Suddenly I can't stop laughing. Put my head under the pillow and go hysterical. I fucking did it. Yeh! Master of the fucking universe. My cock is hard as a steel bar and I think of those pink tits. Think of shoving it down that lipsticked little gob. Up that tight little cunt. Up that tighter little ass. Happy days.

And then I sleep. Like a fucking baby. And when I wake up it's two in the afternoon and the house is silent. Ma at work.

I check Wiki for gulls. Trouble is I didn't pay attention. Seemingly, could be fulmars, cormorants, shags, lesser black-backed gulls, herring gulls, great black-backed gulls, kittiwakes, guillemots, razorbills or black guillemots.

Shags is the best bet. Though razorbills sounds good too. I laugh.

My mobile goes. Fats. Think about not answering. But then ...

He wants to meet. Of course he does. Still pissing himself, I guess.

'You can come here', I tell him. 'Me ma won't be back till dinner time'.

'It's on the news', he says.

'Shut it', I say. You never know who's listening. 'Come over'.

Me ma had left out a bought sponge with lemon filling. She's always leaving stuff like that out hoping I'll eat it, trying to fatten me up. Worried cause I won't eat meat any more. I don't mention it to her but Hitler was a vegetarian too, not because he loved animals (though he did his dog). But it was part of his practise of self control. Which is why I leave the cake to Fats. I'll let me ma think I had some since anyway she won't believe one guy could gobble down so much.

It's on the news all right, one of the lesser items since so far it's regarded as a tragic accident and, as I tell Fats, why would anyone think different. I mean the reality is kind of unbelievable. I can't hardly believe it myself. Maybe the old guy did actually slip and we dreamt the other thing. I try telling Fats that but he just looks at me.

'You're cracked you are, Quentin. Fuckin psycho'. He's smiling as he says it. Still, not a nice thing to say to a friend.

I smile back.

'Kids and all', Fats says. 'Fuckin hell, Quentin. He was father of a family'.

I stick my finger in the lemon cream stuff and lick it. Sickly sweet.

'So?' I say.

'Fuck it'.

'So now it's your turn', I say.

'What?'

'I know you want to', I say. 'Jesus, the buzz I got'. And I tell him about jerking off. 'Best ever'.

Christ almighty, the pig is guzzling down the last morsel of cake.

'Hey Fats, you'll throw up again'.

'Yeah well ... I'm hungry. Stress makes me hungry, like'.

'So you must be permanently fucking stressed. Anyway what d'you think?'

'Fuck, Quentin, leave me alone. I couldn't. I haven't got your ...'

He can't find the word. Limited vocabulary, see.

'Chutzpah', I say helpfully.

'Wha'?'

When she comes home, she can see the cake is all gone and give me a sharp look. She knows I wouldn't have eaten the half of it and when I'm out of the way she'll have a rummage in the waste. It wouldn't be the first time I'd binned stuff. Or maybe she could smell Fats's spliff even though I'd sprayed the kitchen with half a can of Lavender Mist. Thing about me ma is she won't ask something if she's afraid what the answer might be. As if I'd tell her anyway.

'A friend popped by'. There. I've taken pity on her after all. 'We shared the cake'.

She smiles then. Well, keep her sweet.

Then she puts on the six o'clock news. I've seen it already of course.

'Did you hear that, Quentin?' she says even though you'd need to be stone deaf not to, she had it that loud.

'Feller fell off that cliff. Married with young kiddies and all. Shocking'.

'Yeah'.

'That poor, poor family'.

A picture of the old guy at some do in his best gear comes up in the screen.

'Only forty-seven. Shocking it is'.

Me ma is forty-nine so she reckons that's young.

Something occurs to her. 'Isn't that where your party was around there? On the hill'.

'Yeah. So?'

'Well ... nothing. You didn't see anything, then?'

'Ma ... We were at a party'.

'Yes. Well, I just thought ...'

'So how could we see him jump, ma? How?'

'They don't say he jumped. They say tragic accident'.

'Yeah well, they always do, don't they. To protect the family, like'. I'm warming to the theme now. 'Maybe it all got too much. On top of him, like. A moment's madness'.

It was that, all right. Have to stop meself giggling.

Now I know me ma's greatest fear is that I'll top myself. She's always reading about young men who are loners fitting the profile and so on. Also about suicide epidemics. She loves all that stuff, scaring herself shitless. And then of course she thinks maybe it's in the genes, like. See, me old fella hanged himself over the upstairs banisters when I was twelve. It was me found him after school. No way of pretending that was a tragic accident. Blue face, tongue hanging out, stink of piss and that.

'Stupid', I say. 'There's always an alternative'.

'Course there is, Quentin, love. Course there is'.

She's at the cooker. Can't see her face.

'How about a nice omelette for your tea then'.

Eggs. Yuk.

'Ah Jesus, ma, I'm full up with cake'.

'You have to eat healthy food, Quentin'.

'So don't leave cake out then'.

Actually I've just decided to start fasting, but I don't tell her that. Detoxing, isn't that what they call it? Cleansing the system. Getting ready.

I go upstairs and lie on my bed and listen to the Sigur Ros cd I took as a souvenir from the party and stare for ages at the crack in the ceiling that looks like an old man's profile.

Fats has gone all shifty on me. I reckon he's planning to rat me out. Like I said, no one would believe him, but still they might start looking at me different, start watching me. Something will have to be done.

Me ma woke me up last night cause I was yelling in me sleep. Must have been a bad dream only I don't remember it.

Still fasting. Drinking green tea with honey. Don't even want food any more. Bit dizzy at times, but pure and strong.

Yeah, something will have to be done about Fats. To look at him you wouldn't rate him a sentimental fucker but he keeps shaking his head and muttering about the kiddies, the kiddies, just like me ma.

Plan A is to get him to do one as well, partners in crime like. Won't be so keen to shoot off his gob then. But bells'll ring even in certain thick official heads if someone else topples off the cliff walk, so it'll have to be something else. Only trouble is Fats isn't made of the same stuff as me. Goes all coy if I mention it.

'I'd rather not, Quentin', he says like some fucking tightass virgin when you inform her of your wish to poke her.

So it might have to be Plan B after all.

Saw that stuck-up heifer in town today or someone exactly like her. Followed her for a bit thinking, I'll find out where she lives, maybe one of them big houses on the cliff with the dodgy back way in, I can get in some night and do her. But she was clothes shopping with a friend, into one fucking boutique after another, both of them trying things on, short skirts, low tops, laughing their stupid fucking heads off. One place the security guy started giving me funny looks so I gave up. Pity. Enjoyed the fantasy ... well, anyway ...

Tonight me and Fats are going to this club where Fats transacts a regular business. So we'll see.

I admit it. I confess. I broke me fast. Only insofar as I had a couple of vodkas and Red Bull. But on an empty stomach, well. Upshot was the bouncers throw me out. Said I was acting crazy. Fuckers.

Fats comes out too, grumbling cause seems I wrecked his business. Also he was chatting up some heifer, as if any of them would look at him twice unless they were fucking desperate. So anyway he's in a bad mood, which you don't see that often. Or I don't anyway. Too much respect for me, up to now. Another worrying sign.

Anyway, he didn't bring the car out tonight which is why we're freezing our bolloxes off waiting for the last train. I'm grand now after spewing up the drink, still fizzing from the Red Bull. Fats is standing on the edge of the platform with a pissed-off expression on his face and I think, no one about, I could do it now, Plan B, when the train comes, I could do it. And I feel meself getting hard at the thought. Then I notice this kid on the platform, lanky like, long hair, probably plays the fucking violin.

So instead I say to Fats, 'there's one you can do'.

'What?'

'Push him under the train. Then we can leg it'.

He looks at me.

'Go on, you know you want to'.

'I don't'. Then he says, 'Fuck it Quentin, know what, you've lost it. You've fucking lost it, man. You need help'.

Fucking wanker actually said that: you need help.

'If you won't', I say. 'Then I will'.

The train's coming now. I see its lights like big burning eyes. I walk towards the kid.

'CCTV', shouts Fats. 'You're on film here, Quentin. Every fucking thing you do'.

I stop. Fuck. I am losing it, after all. Didn't even think.

I come back.

'Only joking', I said. 'Winding you up'.

He slaps my shoulder then.

'Crazy fucker', he says with a smile.

So here I am in me bed, enjoying not-so-sweet dreams, when me ma comes in her fluffy blue dressing gown looking fucking freaked out.

'It's the guards, Quentin', she says. 'Asking for you. Downstairs. Two guards'.

I'm still half asleep, half thinking it's still a dream.

'What's the time, ma?'

She looks at her watch, 'Just after six …'

'Fuck!'

She flinches from the word like she's been slapped. I don't generally use curse words when she's around.

'Have you done anything, Quentin? Have you?'

'No, ma, nothing'.

'Is it that ... that Richard? Has he got you into trouble?'

I don't say anything, brain going like an express train.

'I knew it …'

'I dunno', I tell her and pull on me jeans. Can't go and meet the cops in me fucking kacks.

A big bald guy and a little greasy-looking one. They're looking at me t-shirt: IN YOUR FACE SUCKERS. Should've thought of that. Kind of funny, though.

'Nothing to smile about here, sonny'.

They want me to accompany them to the station to help with their enquiries. Me ma starts gasping, looks like she's about to have a stroke.

'He's done nothing, me Quentin hasn't', she yells. 'It's that Richard Smyth fella. Bad blood'.

'I'll sort it, ma', I tell her in me soothing voice. I even give her a hug. To look like a good son in front of the cops, despite the t-shirt. She's surprised, and all soft and floppy and warm under that gown. Wish I could stay like that for a bit. In her arms, like.

'Come on, son', the bald cop says.

I'm not your fucking son, I say to meself. But remember, Quentin, cool it.

'Let's go, officer', I say, 'and clear this matter up asap'.

He shoves me head down to push me into the car. Fucker.

So what, I'm thinking? Has fucking Fats ratted me out like I reckoned he would? Has he? Should of tipped the fucker under the train, CCTV or not, lanky kid or not. Should of.

Ok, ok, afternoon of the same day, as they say. I'm staring at a grey door with a little peephole in it, just like in the films, with a thing you can slide across from the outside to look in. So they can check I haven't hanged meself yet. Seems I'm on suicide watch. Yeah right. Like me da, I suppose. Only no one was watching out for him.

So anyway, they're keeping an eye on me. Because, well, I kind of lost it in there, didn't I. One of them actually called me 'obstreperous'. 'Stop being obstreperous, Quentin'. Ha! I should have asked if he knew how to spell it. In fact I think I did, going for him. And then I kind of fainted, probably cause I haven't eaten for three days. They've put food in here but I can't stomach it. Looks like fucking shite. Plastic knife and fork so I can't slit me wrists.

What happened was this. Seems they'd had Fats under surveillance for a while, monitoring his operation was how they'd put it. Went to search his gaff with a warrant and all. Found the gear all right but also a few other items of interest including this fancy camera. A very fancy one. Fats has always been fucking light-fingered.

I can imagine the conversation in me head.

'Didn't think you'd be into photography, Richard'.

Silence.

'Bird-watching, eh. Quite a hobby'.

'Yeah, well ...'

'Trouble is, see, Richard, this here camera is missing property'.

'Yeah well, found it didn't I. Finders keepers, like'.

'That's not how it works, actually ... But tell me now, Richard, where did you find it?

'Can't remember ...'

See Fats has no imagination. Me, I'd have been able to make up some yarn on the spot. Some convincing explanation.

'The cliff walk, eh, Richard. Isn't that where?'

'Might have been'.

'So you admit you were on the cliff walk?'

Fucking ouch.

Fats shrugs.

Up to now, see, the cops don't think they are looking at anything more than theft. Then:

'I didn't do nothin to the fella. I didn't touch him'.

Cops glance at each other. Bells starting to ring in their thick heads.

'What fella is that, Richard?'

'Fella with the camera. Just found it there, like'.

'Right, so how do you know about the fella?'

'On the news, wasn't it. Fella with the kiddies. Slipped off the cliff ...' Fats' eyes furtive, shifting, he's sweating, coming down, fucking putty in their hands.

Upshot is, they land at my front door at fucking 6am and freak out me old ma. Drag me off down to the station just cause Fats couldn't keep his fucking hands off the camera the old guy dropped while falling. Jesus fucking Christ. And I never saw him even pick it up. Shoved it in his fucking Tesco bag, didn't he.

'It was an accident', I say, when it's clear there's no point denying we were there. 'He must have been surprised, like, when we came round the path. Lost his balance. Excited to see all them shags and razorbills, see. Didn't hear us coming and slipped. That's how it was, officer'.

But Fats never thought of that. Turns out he must of already told them the lot. Spilled all the fucking beans. Fucking bastarding wanker. Pointed the finger at me, must of. So that's loyalty for you then. Well two can fucking play at that game, mate.

'It was him', I say, trying to keep the shriek out of my voice. 'He did it', pointing to Fats. 'He pushed the old fella off the cliff just to get his camera ...'

'Oh really?'

'It's true, officer. I'm innocent ... I didn't do nothing'.

'You mean you did something', says the cop, smug smile on his fucking face.

'He did it, the crackhead, fucking alco like all his fucking family. Fat fucking pig did it. Not me. Not me. I begged him to come and report it. I begged him. For the sake of the kiddies ...' I 'm full on shrieking, I know I am. Sweating too, fuck.

Fats is looking at me, tears in his eyes. Jesus.

'Loved you, man', he says. 'I'd never of ... never of ... Loved you ...'

'If what you say is true, Quentin, how do you explain this?' the smug cop asks.

Then slowly, slowly he takes up a smartphone which is lying on the table, Fats's fucking phone, and shows me an image. Some crazy-looking skinny spa pushing an old guy off the cliff edge.

'No', says the cop. 'I didn't take Richard for a photographer but seems I was wrong. Great action shot, isn't it, Quentin'.

It's then I start screaming. Screaming and screaming and screaming. Some fucker calling me obstreperous sent me over the fucking edge. May have fallen to the floor frothing at the mouth for all I remember. Someone shoving a needle in me arm.

And then here and the grey door which someone peeps through every little while. Big burning eyes on him, like the lights of an oncoming train.

Disappearing

It wasn't until after the cat died that May felt herself starting to disappear: without Fluffy to wake her up in the morning demanding breakfast or mewing piteously throughout the day, gazing up at her until May gave in and tossed her a treat; without Fluffy running to the front door when May came home from the shops or church or town, joyfully welcoming her; without Fluffy sitting on her lap in the evenings purring, or sharing her bed, May was starting to doubt if she was there at all.

When Jim had died the previous spring all she had felt was a kind of grim relief, after the sudden shock of his massive stroke had worn off. He had been gardening, digging a patch for the beans. May had glanced up occasionally from the flaky pastry she was making for the apple tart, and there he was, digging, digging, digging. And then suddenly he wasn't. At first she didn't think anything of it. Sometimes, to save coming into the house, he would disappear off into the lilac bushes at the back of the garden to take a pee, a habit she always pursed her lips over. After all, as she'd given up repeating, it wasn't as if he had to climb any stairs: they had a ground floor loo. Jim took no notice. He never did. But on that day, when his bald head and burly body failed to rematerialise, she finally got curious and went to check, only to see him lying stretched out, crushing the variegated tulips. He was snuffling and twitching and his eyes were wild. By the time the paramedics arrived, it was all over.

She had missed him for a while, inasmuch as he wasn't there any more to irritate her or snap at her. The beans remained unplanted and the apple tart never made. He'd always insisted on the meat-and-two-veg-followed-by-dessert kind of dinners his mother had made. But now May mostly lived off omelettes or a chop or even just soup and a sandwich. Pottering about, pleasing herself and the cat. Jim had never liked Fluffy. 'It's looking at me funny', he'd say. Or 'you shouldn't feed it so much. It's getting as fat as you are'. Or, kicking the poor harmless creature, 'get out from under my feet, you stupid fecking eejit', sending Fluffy mewling in terror up the stairs to the bed May hadn't shared with her husband for years.

But now Fluffy had died in a shocking way, under an anaesthetic while routinely having his teeth scaled by the vet. His heart had given out, they said. At his age (ten) and his excessive weight, just a freak occurrence.

And now the house resounded with silence.

And the unnerving suspicion that she herself was fading like a shadow when the sun goes in.

It was the bathroom mirror that started it. All steamed up after May's power shower so that when she looked at herself there was no reflection. It had given her a jolt even though she knew there was a logical explanation and that when she wiped the mirror there she would be after all, a bit smeary and distorted, but substantial enough.

All the same, after that the nagging feeling never left her that, without another living creature to acknowledge her, she had no real substance. She started to talk to herself, softly at first and then more loudly, addressing herself to

'May' as if she were another person who lived in the same house, or even one who was just visiting.

'Well May. Better get a move on and polish the potatoes'.

Or sometimes she, May, would talk to the other person. Sometimes even set out another cup of tea with a biscuit in the saucer for her.

'Drink up, while it's still hot', she'd say. 'Eat your Hob Nob'.

'Get another cat', the person advised her, but she couldn't. Fluffy could never be replaced.

Sometimes she pinched herself to make sure she was still there but gradually it seemed that she couldn't feel the nips as strongly anymore, as if she were going numb. Then she stuck pins in her fingers. This hurt at first and reassured her. But after a while the pain seemed to lessen. The blood seemed thinner.

Outside it was almost worse. As if other people couldn't see her at all, nothing reflected in their eyes when their glances washed over her. Only if she raised her voice in shops did they serve her, looking at her in surprise as if they had only just noticed her existence.

When Jim was alive they had always kept themselves to themselves. Neither of them came from a big family. May's sister, June, lived on the other side of the country and they had almost lost contact. Jim had never liked June and the feeling was mutual.

'That ugly old cow', he called her. 'Face to curdle milk and a voice to strip paint'.

But what he really had against her was that June was argumentative and challenged his assertively-voiced prejudices. 'There's nothing worse than a bossy woman', he'd say. 'No wonder no man would have her'.

For her part June was always telling May to stand up more for herself.

‘He’s a bully’, she said. ‘And a nothing. A big zero’.

There was a lot of truth in that but May didn’t like to hear it from her sister, so they fell out. June hadn’t even come to Jim’s funeral, pleading a prior promise to mind someone’s goldfish or hamster or parrot. So when May phoned her now, her sister was astonished to hear her voice.

‘Are you all right? You sound funny’.

It hadn’t been much of a reassurance. She could tell June was impatient to finish the call, so she did.

As for other friends it was hard to think of anyone she had ever been close to. Truth was she had developed a low tolerance for other people. They were always yakking on about their children or grandchildren or about family acquaintances May didn’t know, or talking about TV shows she hadn’t watched or the doings of celebrities she’d never even heard of. Jim and herself had never been blessed with children, which actually she had come to regard as a blessing since Jim would have made a terrible father. As for TV, Jim had been scathing about the rubbish that was on and, plonked in his big armchair in front of the screen all evening, only watched the news and current affairs programmes as an excuse to snort on about the government or the parlous state of the world. Or else he watched sports, golf, a game he had never played, or boxing, which she couldn’t bear, or GAA, ranting on and on about the inadequacies of various players and managers.

His departure from this world should, she thought, have left her free to do anything she liked. Only she couldn’t think of anything she really wanted to do. Was that all she had been, then … a kind of shadow of her husband? Now when she went to church – her only social outlet – she looked around at the other women of her age, wondering how to engage them in conversation. It seemed, however, that they were always in pairs or little groups absorbed in chit-chat she couldn't bring herself to break into.

When she explained how she felt to the priest she could tell by his tone he didn't understand her. He even laughed, most inappropriately, there in the confession box.

'My dear lady', he said. 'The very fact that you are talking to me proves that you are as real as I am'.

He suggested she go and see her doctor. And also told her to pray. May remembered now that she had never liked this priest, had always found him flippant, with that big insincere smile on his fat lips rabbiting on about the poor and hungry while himself clearly comfortably off and all too glossily well-fed.

She didn't like her doctor either. When she described to him her various aches and pains, her excruciating backaches, her headaches, her stomach aches, any of which could be symptoms of something much more grave, he did no more than prescribe bisodol or paracetamol, which, when she had to pay him €55 for the consultation, seemed like an insult. At the very least he could have sent her for tests. No, she dreaded explaining herself to him.

But then one morning she woke to find that her left arm had vanished. She gazed and gazed, but it just wasn't there. She looked for it under the duvet but no luck, nothing but a crumpled tissue.

It wasn't a huge inconvenience, since she was right-handed and could still manage, but it was certainly disturbing. Reluctantly she dragged herself to Dr Murray. He was a tall, thin, dry-looking man. A grey man, from his still abundant grey hair to his small, grey eyes to his grey complexion to his expensively-tailored grey suit. Even his voice was grey.

'What's the problem?' he asked with a slight sigh. Women of May's age, his demeanour indicated, were forever bothering him with their insignificant problems.

May pointed to where her left arm should be.

'It's gone', she said. 'Went in the night'.

He stared at her absent arm.

'What's gone?' he asked.

'My arm. It was there last night but when I woke in the morning …' May's voice started to break. Oh God, was she about to burst into tears?

'Hmm', he replied. 'You had it yesterday, you say?'

'Certainly. I'd surely have remembered if it wasn't there'.

'Not necessarily. I've heard of cases where people have gone for weeks without noticing a missing body part'.

'Well …' She thought back. Then, triumphantly, 'Last night I threaded a needle and sewed a button back on this coat'. She showed him the very button. A brown plastic one. 'And you can't do that with only one arm'.

'True enough'. Though Dr Murray had never had occasion to sew on a button or sew anything at all, except the odd wound while training as a junior doctor. He noted something on his computer. 'Button', he murmured, as he punched in the keys, adding, 'And you've looked everywhere?'

'Well … not everywhere. I looked where I last had it'.

He folded his hands over his chest. He had very long thin fingers with grey nails. 'Ha! That is to say where you *think* you last had it. But memories, dear lady, are notoriously unreliable. I suggest you go home and have a good hunt around for it, even in places where you think it couldn't possibly be. I for instance am forever laying down my keys, certain they are in a particular place on my desk or the mantelpiece or wherever, only to find them somewhere completely different. Mixed up with dirty socks, or in the sugar bowl, for instance'. He stared at her through his spectacles with those pebble grey eyes of his. 'Or maybe the cat went off with it'.

'The cat's dead'.

'Ah, well … Anyway. Have a thorough look. Take a few paracetamol and if the situation doesn't improve in the next day or two, come back to me and we'll see what we can do. Make that a week …'

He stood up and put out his left hand to shake hers which was confusing since she had awkwardly to grip his with her right.

'Just checking', he laughed greyly.

Back out in the waiting room, May fished out the €55 notes to give to his receptionist, who grabbed them without looking up at her, passing her back a printed receipt.

If May had been hoping that when she woke up the following morning her left arm would have magically returned to her, she was to be disappointed. As instructed by Dr Murray, in her search for the missing arm she had turned the house upside down, as well as she could do anything single-handedly, but no joy. She had been utterly exhausted when finally she sank into bed and, though she dreamed strange dark dreams, the following morning she couldn't remember what they were about, just that she was overcome with an unfathomable sense of oppression.

Two days passed and May couldn't bring herself to go out. On the third day she woke to find her right leg had disappeared from below the knee. She hadn't noticed at first: it was only when she fell getting out of bed that she realised something was amiss. It also seemed that her right hand was becoming more transparent, the brown and gold of the leafy carpet design faintly visible through it, where she pressed down to support herself. No doubt any longer: things were getting serious. Something paracetamol alone couldn't cure.

Getting to the doctor's surgery was quite an ordeal. May had to hop, holding on to railings and lamp posts and even privet bushes as she went, and progress was slow and tiring. Then she found the waiting room full. Mostly with people coughing and spluttering and May feared that on top of everything else she would catch something nasty. When finally her name was called and she hopped down to the inner sanctum where Dr Murray sat, eyes glued to his computer screen, he said rather sharply without looking at her, 'I thought I told you to give it a week'.

'Yes but doctor … things have got worse'.

He managed to look at her then. At least, his eyes passed over where she was standing, as if he couldn't see her at all. Good God, had she disappeared entirely somewhere along the corridor from the waiting room to here? He put on his glasses and then, finally, seemed able to make her out.

'How interesting', he said. 'There's certainly been an acute progression of the disease, if a disease is what it is. Have you been taking your pills?'

'I'm not in pain', May replied. 'Quite the opposite'.

'Well, I don't suppose they would have made any difference. Under the circumstances'. He studied her through the thick glass of his spectacles, eyes narrowed to slits. 'I think we'd better make an appointment for you with a specialist'. He turned back, asking his computer screen. 'But which one? Which one?'

Back home, with a letter in a brown envelope in her hand, a name and telephone number scribbled on it, May sank exhausted into Jim's big armchair. Not a place where she ordinarily liked to sit so that, after the many months since his passing, it was still moulded to the shape of his body. Now it seemed to swallow her up, for, despite what he had always said about her, May wasn't fat and recently had even lost the little flesh she had. The chair was comfortable and comforting, never mind that it seemed to smell faintly of Jim, the pungent carbolic soap he liked to use, disdaining more aromatic products as being suitable only for women and nancy boys. After Jim had gone, the chair had been taken over by Fluffy, and May could smell cat there as well. She snuggled down. She'd make the call to the consultant later, only now she really had to sleep.

Unfortunately, when she woke it was to find that her right hand had disappeared and also her left foot. It would be well nigh impossible now to get to the telephone, let alone key in a number, unless she did it with her nose. But then how would she lift the receiver? The problem was too much for her and she closed her eyes again, almost drugged with the odours rising from the chair.

Spontaneous combustion was ruled out, for after all there was no sign of a fire. Only the last clothes May had worn draped across a big ugly chair that June decided would be the first thing to go into the skip.

Dr Murray, called to give evidence to the coroner, even in the absence of a body, stated that the presumed deceased had been suffering from a rare form of spontaneous evanescence, and when the coroner raised a bushy and interrogatory eyebrow, explained how he himself had witnessed the rapid degeneration of May's bodily presence.

'And that was only the visible bits. God alone could see what was left of her insides'.

'All the same, without a *corpus delicti,* I am somewhat reluctant to issue a death certificate', the coroner stated. 'Maybe the lady just went off somewhere, either deliberately or in a confused state'.

'She couldn't have got far in that case', Dr Murray retorted tartly. 'Since in the absence of a leg she would have had to have hopped'.

June got the house – May never having written her out of her will – and moved back to the city, something she'd always fancied. She got rid of the big armchair but kept most of the other furnishings. As she'd say to anyone who'd listen, not exactly her taste but it would be such a waste to dump them. She bought a blue budgie and called him Jim, diverting herself with arguments with him that she always, triumphantly, won.

In that way June settled down to her new life, and time passed. Being a woman of small imagination, she never seemed to notice the signs of another presence, the little sighs, the fluttering of a curtain or slight displacement of air as if someone had just walked past. Or if she noticed anything at all, June just blew her big nose and put it down to the draughts characteristic of an old house. When Jim squawked at nothing, throwing himself against the bars in agitation, she just threw a blanket over the cage or instructed him not to be so silly.

And when one day she found her keys in the sugar bowl, she just shook her tightly-permed head and chuckled to herself, 'June, June, June, June', she said. 'Whatever will you get up to next?'

So Many Wonderful Things

I read it. Of course I did. You would have too, don't pretend you wouldn't. And no harm either. After all, everyone concerned is dead except me. Oh I know it was marked 'Personal! Keep Out!' with one of those silly little locks on it. A girly sort of a thing that should have made me suspicious from the start. I mean what was Gerry of all people doing with such a yoke and him so much of a man. At least, as much of a man as a nineteen-year-old can be.

A thirty-something-year-old diary found stuffed at the back of my mother's press when I finally brought myself to clear it out after she died. So there it was and I looked at it for a while, with Gerry's doodles all over the outside of it, those funny faces that made us say he was going to be a cartoonist, maybe an illustrator. Because they were good. He was artistic. Not like me. Not like me at all. That's how I knew it was his straight off, the doodles.

My brother Gerry. My big brother. And big he was. Muscular, I mean. Not fat. Good at sports. An all-round good guy. A high-achiever. The apple of his mother's eye. Not like me. Well, they say boys are always their mother's favourites, don't they? A girl can't compete with that. But I wasn't Daddy's girl either. That was reserved for Rose, the baby. I fell in the middle, the margarine in the sandwich, and after what happened, fell out altogether. After what I always thought had happened.

We lived in a suburb on the unfashionable north side of Dublin. An ordinary family, as people might have described us, in a three-bedroomed semi. But who is ever ordinary when you come down to it? I can never get over people who are happy to describe themselves as such when, in fact, isn't everyone extraordinary? The things that happen to people. Or if nothing much happens, that's amazing too.

My father was a foreman in a factory, my mother didn't work outside the home. They were good enough Catholics in that my mother went to church every week and my father sometimes. They went through all the appropriate motions anyway and listened to priests at a time when priests were still held in awe. Before all the scandals, that is. But even after the scandals my mother, widowed by then, never, as she put it, believed the lies people told about the priests. Yes, there was a rigidity about their religion that made me a pariah at age seventeen when I got pregnant. Until I was hustled into a marriage with Jimmy.

'You don't have to, Elaine', Gerry kept saying to me. 'You really don't have to'.

But it was either that or give up the baby, there were no alternatives for a young girl in trouble then. And Jimmy was ok. He still is even though we aren't together any more. But that was all my fault, as things usually are. Or will I now have to revise that judgement in the light of …

Yes, Gerry was my slightly older brother and Rose came after me, almost as fast. Gerry was always handsome, even when going through puberty, when most boys get spotty and smelly. Rose was a little doll with golden curls and pink cheeks. Me, I was awkward and gangly, sallow-skinned and mousey-haired. Plain Elaine, they called me.

Sullen, sulky, was what I heard I was. And when you get told the same thing over and over, aged eight, nine, ten, eleven, it has an effect. Of course it does.

I was clever though. And did well at school until I fell in with what my mother and father called 'a bad lot'. Aged thirteen, out drinking and smoking and letting my small breasts be groped by anyone except Martin Pratt in the waste ground beyond the estate, so that one time a gang of us were caught and hauled back by the juvenile liaison officer and my father smacked me on the head and said he'd send me to the industrial school if I didn't mend my ways.

I didn't mend anything but was more careful after that. I lost my cherry, as we girls put it, to Keith Price when I was fourteen, and it was only thanks to very good luck and clingfilm that I didn't get pregnant right away.

But I didn't mean to go on about any of that, not about me. That's all past and gone anyway and although my parents called me wild, I wasn't really, never took drugs for instance. Just wild in their eyes. Rose was much wilder, only they never knew about any of that, didn't want to know, until she crashed off the rails altogether. No, to look at me now you'd say I was an ordinary mother of two, young grandmother of one, albeit separated, but who isn't these days.

I was going to explain about Gerry and his diary but first I suppose I should say what happened that day, that night. What I thought happened.

Gerry was always protective of me. He told my father to leave off hitting me, for instance, after they found out about the baby. He stood up for me and I adored him. So then come my wedding day and my mother was bustling about, pretending she'd never said all those awful things to me, pretending it was the happiest day of her life. She had even bought a fancy hat to squash down the steel wool of her perm. My father didn't say much, he never did, unless angry. That day he smelt of whiskey from early morning. I wished it was Gerry rather than my father who was going to give me away.

It wasn't a big do. Not under the circumstances. Neighbours came to the church out of curiosity I suppose, to see how far gone I was. But baby was tiny and even at four months I didn't show much, especially in the loose dress I wore, so the ould wans must have been disappointed. We had a meal with both immediate families in the Shieling, prawn cocktail or soup, chicken or salmon, profiteroles. I felt too sick to eat much. Jimmy was red-faced and hung over after his stag and hardly said a word. He was always a quiet fellow, and when Keith Price came up to us at the afters with a nasty grin on his face and asked if Jimmy was sure the baby was his, it was Gerry who faced up to him.

But that wasn't it. That was nothing.

Although thinking about it now, I'm remembering how Pricer had turned on Gerry and muttered something I hadn't understood at the time, before Gerry pushed him out.

'What did he say?' I asked.

'Nothing, rubbish. He's a prick'.

And we left it at that. I think we did.

As I said, I was feeling sick so when I started drinking, as I had to, to get through the thing, those Bacardis and Coke went straight to my head. I still don't know what I was supposed to have said to Gerry but at some point very late in the night he stormed out, as I was later told, drove to Bull Island and drove his car into the sea. Some wedding night, heh?

It had to have been my fault. That's what I was told. That's what I always believed. That's why, apparently, everything bad afterwards happened. Rose going bonkers on drugs, my father's stroke and death several years after. That's what my mother was still telling me while I was caring for her in her last terrible years. That it started that night, or rather, it started when I lost all respect for myself and let myself get fucked. Only she didn't use that word, of course.

It almost killed me to think that. To think that my last words to my brother were angry or mocking or whatever, enough to send him over the edge.

'Of course, the McCarthys were always a mad lot', my mother once said after my father's death, referring to his side. 'Mental cases, alcoholics'.

Not to excuse me, of course. Just to deny that she had any part of it.

It's not fair, is it, when people die before they can be called to account for what they've done. Child abusers, for instance. Sometimes I really hope there's a hell after all, so they can rot in it. Those medieval pictures of torments, well, it's too good for some people. Not that I would really wish that on my mother or even my father. In their case it was thoughtless ignorance spiked with a self-protective blindness. If it wasn't that, then it was truly wicked, and I don't want to believe that even of them.

I hold my brother's diary in my hands. I have closed it now though the broken lock won't shut properly. I am wondering what to do with it. It's only me now who might care what it says, only me who cares about Gerry. I suppose I could show it to Jimmy but I think he'd only shrug and make little of it. He never realised just how badly I was affected by it all.

I open the diary again and read the first line in my brother's spiky handwriting: '1978 in which so many wonderful things are going to happen'. He was left-handed and it always looked awkward whenever he wrote anything.

Now there's a thing. A tear blotting the page. When was the last time I wept?

I flip over the pages and see how much he loved, my big brother, how he was swept away having found out what love is all about. Young love, first love. Something I missed out on, that first rush of joy and the wonder of lovingly discovering another's naked body. It wasn't like that on the waste ground behind the estate.

Why he felt he had to tell, I can't imagine. Did he really think they'd be ok about it? Or maybe it was dangerously near not being a secret any more. I thought of Keith Price's remark at my wedding. What had he called my brother, softly, with that nasty grin on his face? Mrs Murphy?

Charlie Murphy and my brother. Madly, illegally in love. And Gerry, as the diary reveals, has him agonising and finally deciding to tell my mother. Well, actually he blurts it out when she starts going on at him, as I remember she often did, about not having a girlfriend. He blurts it out one night when he comes home, a few drinks on him, rosy from kisses. Charlie Murphy who died later in a motorbike crash.

How could he be so foolish as to think she'd understand, not to mention forgive? My father, when she told him, freaked out completely, of course. His son a nancy-boy, a shirt-lifter, a poof! It couldn't be. It wouldn't be. Either get over it and be normal or get out and never ever come back. I could imagine it all. My father in a rage was a sight to see, especially with the whiskey on him.

That's how it must have been at my wedding. My father in a whiskey rage and nothing promised by Gerry. Because he couldn't and wouldn't. I see him, my lovely brother jumping into his car, the drink on him too, dangerously so. Blinded by angry tears. Careering down the road, over the causeway to the island and out into the icy sea.

And they never said. Never even hinted. They let me think it was my fault. And now, well, I'm sitting here with the diary on my lap and I can't get my head around it at all. I just can't.

NOT IN FRONT OF THE CHILDREN

Why couldn't we have had a family holiday like everyone else? Goosepimpled on the beaches at Tramore or Lahinch, or knee-deep in mud at the grandparents' farm. Or if we had to go abroad, why not simply sun ourselves in Majorca or Torremolinos or Lanzarote?

My parents always had to be different: my beautiful mother, with her famous 'style', my father with the piratical patch over one eye and limp he had won in some far-flung war, his elegant cane now sported like a trophy. How I suffered from it all. It turned me into the scowling eleven-year-old I was, given to alternate sulks and tantrums, the year we boarded the big plane and flew for hours over the ocean, changing to a smaller plane somewhere or other and finally arriving at a dirt runway set among wooded mountains.

I gasped when I stepped out. Wet heat socked me in the guts and I trickled on to the red dust. My mother and father shook someone in uniform by the hand and called me over.

'What a cutie pie', the man said in a fake American accent. I scowled. I was anything but cute and I knew it. He laughed not nicely, like he knew it too, and all the medals on his chest rattled together.

This was the general. My father had fought with him in the war that earned the eye patch and the limp and, years on, the general had invited my parents to visit the small state which he now governed.

I looked out of the tinted windows of the limousine that was taking us to our residence, at the houses made, it seemed, of corrugated iron and cardboard, at the dirty and near-naked children who stared blankly at us, the adults who turned away, and I wished I was with Sally Fannin in Butlins Mosney riding on the roller coaster.

I wished it even more later when I discovered there was nothing for me to do. There were no other guests. No children, no women, except servants. It was pointed out to me as I sulked and raged that there were tennis courts. But I couldn't play tennis and anyway didn't have a partner, apart from the odd occasion when my mother put on the trim whites that suited her so well and knocked a ball to me, for me to miss or send rocketing over the wire fence, there to be retrieved with alacrity by one of the many good-looking young officers watching us. There was a swimming pool, too, into which I dutifully splashed. But again, without friends it was no fun. My mother sometimes accompanied me, wearing a pretty swimsuit, lowering herself into the pool and smiling at the spectators before launching into a dignified breast-stroke that kept her coiffed head high out of the water.

After a few minutes she would emerge, droplets sparkling on her skin like diamonds, and one or two of the young officers would join her at the poolside for a long drink with leaves in the glass. I would be encouraged to stay in the water and 'enjoy myself'. Mostly though I'd follow my mother out and sit dripping on the edge, splashing my feet sullenly in the water until a waiter brought me a drink with leaves in it, too.

'Your very own cocktail, baby', my mother laughed, sharing the joke with the young man.

At such times my father was 'with the general', not to be disturbed, shut up in an office that smelt of leather and cigars.

In the evenings after dinner, before I could decently be sent up to the bedroom I had all to myself, crammed with heavy mahogany furniture and dusty drapes, I would perch on an upholstered chair in what the general was pleased to call the games room, a picture book on my lap, dangling skinny legs that ended in white ankle socks and patent leather shoes, glaring at the adults. Occasionally I was allowed play chess with my father, but more often his adversary was a fat colonel with a shiny bald head.

My mother, glorious in evening dress, would thumb through the 78s and occasionally let out a yelp of delight. One of the young officers, or more often the general himself, would install the record she chose on the phonograph and then gallantly extend a hand to ask her for the pleasure of the next dance.

The night in question started like this, like all the others. It was close to the end of the third week of our stay and I was bored out of my mind. Maybe the adults were too, my mother anyway. We had been confined to the residence, apart from a couple of trips to a mountain resort surrounded by armed soldiers, where we could play tennis or swim in the pool or drink long cool drinks with leaves in them. My mother had been told there was nothing to see in the city, no shops worth the bother, and in any case it was unsafe for us to be wandering about on our own. My father was, meanwhile, still spending his days ensconced with the general in the study.

Earlier that day, my parents had had words. I had heard snatches of the row from my room when I was having my siesta.

'You don't know what it's like for me', my mother was screeching.

My father mumbled.

'Don't keep saying that. I can't stand it any more'.

Mumble, mumble.

Loud sobs and my father suddenly shouting, 'don't push me too far, Margot. I know what's been going on'.

'I do too, Howard. Still playing your stupid war games'.

More yells and then – but could I believe my ears? – a sharp crack followed by silence. I pulled the pillow over my head.

At dinner my mother was pale but composed. And stunningly beautiful in aquamarine satin. My father, older-looking, grey-skinned, his limp seeming more pronounced as he leaned on his cane. Had he hit her? Had she hit him? Had one of them fired a gun?

After the feast we adjourned as ever to the games room. On this particular evening for some reason none of the young officers were in attendance. The chess set was pulled out and the bald colonel wedged his bottom down opposite my father. My mother, who had drunk a lot of wine with her dinner and who was now sinking cocktails – they all were – cooed as usual over the record collection. I pulled a large picture book at random out of the rack. The foxtrot began.

When my mother sat down to enjoy a cigarette, the general wheezed over to me.

'Perhaps the little lady would like to dance, too'.

The little lady didn't want to but 'no' apparently wasn't a word this man understood. He grabbed my hand and yanked me from my seat. His jacket was unbuttoned, his shirt open, and when he pulled me against him some necklace that he was wearing pressed painfully into my cheek. At the end of the dance I stumbled away and buried my scowling face in the book.

It was full of dirty pictures. It had women with giant breasts suckling monkeys, it had dogs with women, snakes. It showed girls and boys kneeling before men with big thingies like the one I had felt through the general's trousers.

When I looked up, he was dancing with my mother again. He was shorter than she, his face against her neck. Her eyes were shut. The room was heavy with smoke and heat and the sticky smell of the cocktails. My fingers left damp patches on the book.

'Knight takes Queen', called the fat colonel.

Suddenly my father started shouting.

'You're cheating'. He swept the chess pieces to the floor. 'You always cheat, you ...' And he used a bad word.

'Pas devant les enfants', warned my mother but it was too late.

The fat colonel yelled and my father pushed him over, chair and all. He slapped my mother's face. The general said something sharp to my father in his own language, looked at my mother and then started laughing. Not nicely.

My father went wild. He seized his cane and surprised everyone but me by drawing a sword from it. He lurched over to the general and drove the sword right through him. The laughter turned to a gurgle. Blood spurted from that bare chest. When the colonel, who by now had extricated himself from his chair, pulled out a gun, I jumped up behind him and thumped him hard on his baldy head with the dirty pictures. He keeled over.

My mother was screaming, on her knees. My father shouted more bad words and raised the sword again but just then several young officers burst into the room, grabbing my father and dragging him away. My mother threw herself across the body of her dancing partner who, alas, would foxtrot no more. When they raised her up I noticed that the necklace he wore was made of teeth strung together. Teeth just like mine and yours.

Later, my hysterical mother was explaining to the police chief a version of what had happened. I could see that he was taken with her even though her aquamarine dress was now stiff with the general's blood and her hair and make-up a mess. He touched her bare arm and said everything would be all right, leave it to him.

True to his word, he got us on to a plane and out to a safe haven in a few hours, despite the curfew. At the last minute my father was bundled on with us, his skin greyer than ever, despite the cuts and bruising, and his eye patch was missing, showing an empty and scrunched up socket. He seemed to have difficulty getting words out, but my mother wasn't talking to him anyway.

If you read about it now, you will learn that my father was heroically instrumental in ridding the country of a tyrannical regime that was planning further atrocities. He had even, so they said, been prepared to sacrifice self, lovely wife and young daughter to a nobler cause. Happily it hadn't come to that. The assassination provoked a popular uprising after which a democratic leader was elected. That's what the history books say. All I know is that we arrived back home to a welcome for stars – hundreds of people at the airport, flashing lights and shouted questions. My breathtaking mother smiled and waved and later appeared on the front pages of all the newspapers, my father huddled in his wheelchair. I remembered how the police chief had whispered to me that if I ever said what I had really seen a man would come in the night and cut out my tongue, so I pretended that I had lost my memory. People felt sorry for me and thought I was in shock. Later I saw the police chief in other newspaper pictures standing behind the ear of the democratically elected leader.

Now all the witnesses but me are gone. The bald colonel was executed by the new regime. My father died within months of his return. Was he a hero, a villain or a fool? I didn't know. My mother never said. She started giving dancing classes and married one of her pupils, a man with a ginger wig. I was sent to boarding school and there learned that the newlyweds had died in an avalanche while skiing.

Years later I again flew over the ocean to the little state. I gasped at the wet heat, shook hands with a man in a suit and got into a limousine from the airport, now tarmacadamed. I was driven to the city past houses made of corrugated iron and cardboard. Naked, dirty children looked up and adults turned away.

The occasion was the naming of a street after my father, the unveiling of a statue. I had been invited as the only surviving member of the family. Over cocktails, a bemedalled colonel told me that he remembered how my mother and I had played tennis, how we had swum in the pool. He had been a young officer then.

'Your mother was very beautiful', he sighed. 'How differently things might have turned out'.

I wondered what he meant but didn't ask in case a man would come to cut out my tongue.

We clinked glasses. The colonel didn't ask me to dance. I wasn't beautiful like my mother.

Later that year there was a military coup. My father's street was renamed over again and his statue destroyed.

Roadblocks

I couldn't do it myself, so I hired a hitman. Then I called Eithne to meet for lunch. My alibi. After the meal, I would bring her back to the house on some pretext so we could find the body together. That way no one would suspect me of a thing. All very straightforward, as you might think.

And it would probably have gone to plan if I hadn't hired the most idiotic hitman in the whole of Dublin. Geeks Molloy was someone I'd met in a rough pub with my brother, one of his shadowy associates. We'd all gotten drunk together and Geeks had confided some incriminating information to me regarding knees and sledgehammers and suchlike under the misapprehension that, like my brother, I was attracted to people from that world, to Geeks himself, skinny, grey-skinned and hollow-eyed, with a shaven head that sported a tattooed swastika.

After that night I would notice him from time to time shuffling around the inner city looking furtive. I don't know if he remembered what he'd told me but he always greeted me with a cool 'howaya, missus!' So when I was looking for someone to do the job, Geeks sprang instantly to mind.

He was a bit bemused, but up for it. Half the money now and half after, I said. I'd watched enough TV crime dramas to know that was the way to do it. And I wasn't entirely stupid. I left the back door open but locked away all my valuables in advance, not to put temptation in Geeks' way.

Eithne and I went to the little Japanese restaurant on the quays. I ordered a vegetarian Bento box because I don't believe in eating living creatures. That is to say, creatures who have once lived. Eithne had a huge bowl of seafood soup and I tried to avoid looking at the things bobbing in it, prawns and mussels and other fishy invertebrates, as well as some unidentifiable chunks of what may or may not have been plant life and long tapeworms of noodle. Of course she asked about Algie and I replied brightly that he was grand, all the time wondering how Geeks would do the deed. Was he at that very moment smothering his victim with a pillow or perhaps manually strangling him? I had told him to make it look natural, no guns or knives or ligatures. And preferably, because after all I am humane at heart, painless.

'Are you ok?' Eithne asked in alarm.

I was choking on a lump of wasabi.

'Wow', I croaked. 'That stuff is hot'.

After the meal, we wandered into a bookshop. Eithne was drawn to the shelves of macabre titles – she is into bloody murder in a big way, strange for someone in ordinary life so prim and gentle – but I leaned to the travel section. Now, I was thinking, at last nothing to tie me down any more, the world will be my oyster. I felt myself becoming light-headed at the notion and thumbed through rough guides to Eritrea and Cambodia and Costa Rica.

I lured her back to the house with a promise of the loan of a rare DVD of *Nightmare Alley*. I had seen it in Laser the previous week and snapped it up, knowing she wouldn't be able to resist.

My little road looked as boringly respectable as ever, as uneventful, my house as inscrutable. The net curtains, I suddenly noticed, perhaps not as fresh-looking as they might be.

Eithne was babbling on about some Slovenian or Slovakian man, I wasn't clear which, who had started a conversation with her in Eason's café.

'I immediately felt a connection, Barbara', she was saying.

But I was distracted by the sight of Geeks, lurking at the end of the street. Had something gone wrong? Or, Good Lord, did the idiot think I was going to pay him there and then? Where Eithne couldn't see, I made a brushing away sign with my hand.

'He gave me his mobile number'.

Geeks was looking from my face to my hand and back and eventually got the message because he turned on his heel and slunk round the corner.

'What do you think?'

'Er …'

'Should I ring him? I mean, Barbara, there was a definite connection'.

'Mm …'

'Angela says he's only after an Irish passport'. Angela was Eithne's married younger sister, a begrudging kind of a person by all accounts.

'Could be …'

She looked downcast. We were approaching the front door.

'Still', I said, collecting myself. 'No harm in meeting him again on neutral ground and see if you really hit it off'.

'Yes', Eithne's somewhat puddingy face lit up and we entered the house in jovial mood.

Not a sound. We went into the kitchen. Nothing.

'So where's Algie then?' Eithne asked.

'Er …' I looked around vaguely.

'Algie', Eithne called. He was a firm favourite of hers.

No reply. She looked at me.

'That's strange', I said. 'Very strange. Algie?', I called as well, my voice trembling a tad. 'Maybe he went out'.

'Went out?' She of course looked at me as if I were mad.

'Anyway', I said, putting the kettle on. 'Tea?'

'Yes, please, but I need the loo'.

Eithne gone, I glanced in the front room, the back, no Algie, alive or dead. Maybe, I thought, Geeks had kidnapped him and was holding out for more money.

But then a scream from upstairs. I raced to see, already knowing. Eithne was standing at the open door of the bathroom. I peered beyond her.

'Oh my God!'

Was it Eithne or I who exclaimed? Or both of us. In any case I had no need to dissemble shock and surprise. I was genuinely aghast at the sight of the lifeless form floating in the tub.

'Algie!' I cried, throwing myself forward and pulling my best friend from the cooling water. 'Algie!'

Eithne was looking at me, pity and dismay on her face, mixed with deep puzzlement.

'But how exactly', she asked, 'could a dog of that size climb into a bath and drown in it?'

Let me get this straight once and for all. I adored my terrier mongrel, just as before him I had adored his mother Tess, our family pet. But Tess had died at the reasonable age of twelve after a happy life of snuffling through bushes, chasing squirrels and burying bones. Algie was one of the two surviving pups of Tess's late middle-aged first pregnancy, delivered by caesarean section (she had been six, partner unknown, though suspicion rested firmly on a randy local mutt). We decided to keep him and for nearly seven more years the two of them gambolled, played and fought happily together, both mother and son neutered to avoid any shocking carry on. When I moved into my own house I took Algie with me. But he was now seventeen and showing no sign of wanting to depart to the great kennel in the sky. Still quite peppy in fact, although cataracts impeded his vision and deafness his hearing. And then there were the irremovable black stains on the pale wooden floor of my new kitchen extension where Algie nightly, and daily now as well, emptied his incontinent bladder. Added to which were the occasional plops of poop and piles of sick from eating something nasty in the park. At least with the sick he was quite likely to gobble it up again and save me having to wipe up the worst.

I had put up with this state of affairs with saint-like fortitude, longer, I reckon, than most. No longer, however, than considered reasonable by my dog-owning co-walkers who met at eleven every morning to complete several circuits of the park, while all possible permutations of canine life tore around them. These people were fanatics. One had even started a website dedicated to 'The Eleven O'Clockers', posting news and pictures of our four-footed friends odiously saccharine in their sentimentality. I really had very little in common with them, but – call me pathetic – since I had been made redundant and was now working from home translating scientific and technical papers of incalculable tedium, my social circle had shrunk considerably. The changed circumstance brought home to me, in fact, how many of the people I had considered bosom buddies were in fact mere acquaintances I could have a laugh with after work. Only Eithne survived from that time and even she, I suspected, liked Algie more than she liked me. My dog-walking companions at least got me out of the house and into daily conversation with people who knew and cared nothing about polysaccharides, polypeptides and polynucleotides.

But whenever I mentioned Algie's decline to any of them, they would pat him on the head and comment 'bless him', or some such, often adding 'he looks as if he's got a good few years left in him yet'. Words that struck an icy blast to my soul.

I am nearly forty-three. Any hopes of children of my own fast fading now, though to be perfectly honest being a mammy has never really attracted me. But with advancing age, I am becoming ever more aware of my own mortality and it came to me quite recently over a large glass of Rioja, my second or third, accompanied by some maudlin Leonard Cohen songs, that what I really want to do with the time remaining me is squeeze the most out of every moment and that scooping poop and swabbing pee do not in any shape or form enter this plan. I want to fill the goblet of experience to the brim and then drain it to the very dregs. Or at least that was the revelation inspired by Lenny and the Rioja. In the sober light of day, thundering headache notwithstanding, I decided I would just like to travel, to meet new people, to have at least one more passionate encounter before I die (haven't had one of those since I was thirty-eight and Brian, married, staid and seriously overweight, wasn't actually that passionate).

The roadblock, as I saw it, was poor Algie. Given his physical condition, it would be over and above to ask anyone, even the devoted Eithne, to look after him if I decided to go away for any length of time. At least, as my dog-loving chums kept telling me, he wasn't suffering. If only he were, I secretly thought. Then I could take him to the vet with a clear conscience and have him humanely – that word again – put down. But a dog who still enjoys snuffling in bushes, burying bones all over my garden, digging them up again and burying them somewhere else, as well as chasing squirrels and cats he can't see but can smell perfectly well, still has a quality of life. No denying it. That was when the notion came to me of the hitman, and Geeks in particular. At one fell stroke, I thought, I would be free.

My dog-loving chums – I had to go and tell them the sad news – were full of sympathy for my loss. Simon, he who had developed the Eleven O'Clockers website, got quite carried away at the prospect of a funeral with all the trappings, the other dogs attending with mourning bands on their left front legs and so on, and so was devastated when I had to inform him that the vet had already disposed of Algie.

'What about the ashes?' Simon asked.

'Er …'

'You should have asked for the ashes at least', Simon said reproachfully. 'We could have had a ceremonial scattering'.

But Mairead, brisk owner of two airhead red setters, defended me. 'How could Barbara even think straight at such a traumatic time?'

I nodded, trying to look traumatised. However, I was thinking sideways of Geeks, the eager way he had taken the balance of my money and the way he had asked, hopefully, if there was anything, anyone else I wanted disposed of.

'Well', he'd added cheerfully when I demurred, 'ye know where ye can find me, missus, whenever ye need to', squeezing my arm and leering.

'Why in heaven's name the bath?' I'd legitimately asked as he shambled away. But he was already gone.

The irony was that my life started to seem even emptier after the passing of Algie. No dozing creature lying under my feet as I worked at my desk. No hopeful little face staring blindly up at me whenever I passed the box of dog biscuits or carved off a chunk of cheese for myself. It had been uncanny the way, despite being deaf, he could always seem to hear the opening of the fridge door or the rustle of a food wrapper. Conditioned, like Pavlov's dog myself, I would eye the clock at ten to eleven, and once even went and picked up Algie's lead, only then remembering with a heavy heart that it was now redundant. I couldn't bring myself to throw the thing in the bin and sat down with it in my hands, eyeing my ghostly reflection beyond the formulae and equations on the computer screen, the German text I had been labouring to turn into appropriate English. A tear actually ran down my cheek. Oh God, what had I done?

The trouble with brochures is the embarrassment of riches contained within them. How to choose Sardinia over Corsica? Lebanon over Turkey? New York over San Francisco? Tunisia over Morocco? Thailand over Indonesia? The world was now indeed my oyster but actually I'd never eat an oyster to save my life, would indeed gag at the prospect. I was frozen into indecision.

Eithne caught me thumbing through said brochures when she returned *Nightmare Alley*.

'Holiday plans?' she asked.

'Well ... I thought it might take my mind off things'.

'Hmm'.

Was it my guilty conscience or did she seem cool?

I had to break the silence.

'I suppose poor Algie must have had a stroke or something, to climb into the bath like that'.

'And did he turn on the taps and fill the tub first?'

Very cool.

'I ... I must have forgotten to drain it after I went out. Er. I was running a bit late'.

'Hmm'.

'Did you like the film?'

'Not really. Too much gratuitous violence'.

I thought people who watched films like that and read the sort of books Eithne read enjoyed gratuitous violence.

'I mean, biting the heads off live chickens ...'

'A step too far, I agree'.

'Any cruelty to dumb animals is anathema to me, Barbara. In my opinion, people who commit such crimes should be locked up and the key thrown away'. Upon which words, and with a hard glint in her eye as she looked at me, Eithne swept out.

I felt so down after my best friend turned against me that I wandered to the park to join the Eleven O'Clockers, even without the legitimacy of a dog to take with me. The pity I saw on all faces moved me to tears again and Mairead clasped me to her bosom while her jealous setters leapt up at us barking. But even as I nearly fainted from the tightness of Mairead's embrace and the pungency of her perfume and body odour, I imagined how all this love would turn to scorn and disgust if Eithne ever opened her big mouth.

They say the second time around is easier. I don't know if it was for Geeks but it certainly was for me. I didn't experience the slightest twinge of conscience, but then again I had always been more fond of Algie than Eithne, whose incessant old maidenly fussing got on my nerves. The funeral service everyone agreed was lovely, the priest intoning lots of kind words about the deceased and even including a useful health and safety element in his homily since Eithne's demise had been due to a tragic, not to say freak accident, a plugged-in electric hairdryer falling into the bubble bath in which she was reclining. ('What is it with you and baths?' I asked Geeks when I handed over the agreed amount. He just shrugged, grinned, rubbed his swastika and gave back the key Eithne had entrusted to me in case she ever locked herself out). Angela, the sister, black moustache and all, struck a sour note by suggesting that Eithne might have had drink taken when she took the bath and that this had clouded her judgement. She was after all, quoth Angela, a lonely and love-starved spinster. It was with extreme difficulty I held back from leaping up to defend my friend against such an unwarranted slur. Then Angela's daughter Sarah Jane struck more sour notes when she sang the *Ave Maria* with such an excruciating wobble that several babies started to scream. Still and all, it was a nice send-off and the church was full.

We were all standing outside in the spring breeze waiting for the departure of the hearse to the cemetery and shaking our heads at the fickle finger of fate, when I noticed a swarthy and muscular man in his mid-thirties staring at me. He soon disappeared off into the crowd and I dismissed him from my thoughts, only to have to re-admit him into them at the graveside. He was definitely staring at me and not at all in a pleasant way.

The priest said what was necessary and people threw mementoes into the grave (for want of anything better, I threw in the *Nightmare Alley* DVD. God knows I didn't want to keep the damn thing). Then we moved away. I tried to attach myself to someone, anyone, but I didn't really know Eithne's family and friends, except Angela to see, and she was in the middle of a grim-faced bunch of people. The swarthy man slunk up to me as I somehow knew he would.

'I am Marko', he said, with a strong Eastern European accent.

'Are you?'

'Eithne told you maybe'.

'No, I'm afraid not'.

'Well, Miss Barbara. She told me about you. Lots of things'. His tone of voice wasn't friendly even though he was smiling. I noticed some of his teeth were gold-capped.

A suspicion dawned. 'Are you Slovakian?' I asked.

'No. I am from Ptuj'.

'Where?'

'Slovenia'.

The man from Eason's. Eithne must have phoned him after all.

'We must talk'.

'I don't see why we should'.

'Because, Miss Barbara, we have a lot to talk about'. And he tapped his nose in a sinisterly suggestive way.

Somehow I couldn't see Marko letting himself be disposed of in a bath. This time, it wouldn't be so simple.

I blame Geeks. Evidently he had become complacent. 'No problemo', he had said when I outlined the assignment to him, stressing the physical attributes of what we in the business call the goner. 'Bring him on'. Maybe the drugs he bought with his new earnings had made him reckless. Anyway, I was starting to wonder why I hadn't heard from him despite the hefty advance (his price was going up), when, a week later, my brother called suggesting a drink. Something he did from time to time, usually with me buying unless he'd had a winning streak on the ponies or poker.

We met in the same rough pub where he had first, fatefully, introduced me to Geeks. It was therefore perfectly natural for me to ask after our friend. My brother shook his head.

'Drowned', he said.

'In the bath?' It popped out. My brother gave me a look.

'In the Liffey', he said. 'Fell off the Ha'penny Bridge'.

Now, how could that happen, I wondered, the same footbridge having cast iron railings that had to be at least five feet tall.

'Suicide?' I whispered hopefully.

My brother looked at me again with scorn. 'Geeks top himself? I don't think so. Probably trying to walk on water. He was high as a kite, seemingly'.

Of course, I thought, how could I, or Geeks himself, with his wasted frame that might be able to overcome an elderly dog of medium size or even an overweight middle-aged woman reclining in a bubble bath, imagine he could get the better of a fit young man bulging with muscle, who had probably done military service to boot? I decided to book myself an extended holiday to some remote location as soon as possible and meanwhile spent the night in a hotel in case I went back to find an unwelcome visitor lurking in my little house.

All, however, seemed as boringly respectable as ever the following morning as I made my way up my street. And, I thought, walking up the garden path, I really must remember to wash those curtains.

The house had been stripped. Where pictures had been removed from the walls were now pale patches. The TV was gone. Also the music centre, the microwave and the PC that was my meal ticket.

While I was gasping in horror at the sight, my landline rang. *Withheld* came up on the screen. I thought for a second then answered.

'Miss Barbara', came the deep accented voice. 'You are home at last?'

'Marko', I said. 'Are you responsible for this atrocity?'

'What?'

'You've taken all my things!' I glanced at yet another bare patch on the wall. 'Even my autographed photograph of Patrick Swayze!'

'What? You crazy woman! What you say?'

'If not you, then who?'

'We need to talk ...'

'Oh for God's sake. I've been robbed and you want to talk!'

'I come instantly'.

And he hung up.

I sat on the floor. Even though my IKEA rocking chairs had been left me, I didn't feel like rocking just then. To lose Patrick Swayze twice, once to cancer and now to some sneak thief was really too much. I started to sob.

Suddenly I experienced a horrible wet and slobbery sensation on my face. I opened my eyes and there was ...

'Algie!'

Had the ghost of my beloved pet returned in my time of need? My pet as he had been when a young pup.

Then I heard merry laughter and looked up. Standing over me were Simon and Mairead.

'The door was open', said Mairead. She looked around. 'What's happened here?'

'I've been robbed'.

'Have you informed the proper authorities?' asked Simon.

I shook my head. 'I'm only back', I said.

Simon busied himself with his mobile phone.

All the time I found myself caressing the puppy. It's true what they say. Dumb animals really do have a calming effect.

'This little fellow is Zeus', Mairead said. 'I saw him at the animal sanctuary and thought he was the living spit of poor Algie'.

'He's very like'.

'I'm so glad you've taken to him. He was due to be put down if we didn't find a home for him'.

'A home! But I can't. I'm going away'.

'Oh ...' And then 'Holy God!' A looming darkness had filled the doorway, inspiring Mairead's outburst. Marko.

'Yes, I see it is truth how you have been robbed'. He looked around, the picture of innocence and, in his swarthy way, actually rather good-looking.

'The guards are on their way', I said pointedly.

'Good, good', he said, rubbing hairy hands. 'If you don't like to talk to me, I can talk to them'.

The robbery had made me forget the moot point.

'This is nice house', he went on conversationally. 'I look for new place to live. Maybe I move in here'.

'You've got some cheek', I said.

He looked at the patches on the walls. 'Of course, needs decoration, but I am handy man. Very handy'. He smiled, flashing gold.

'Who is this?' Simon asked, now off the phone. 'Is he annoying you, Barbara?'

He was obviously trying to stand up to Marko, but failing miserably. Simon, we all agreed behind his back, was a nerd and a wimp. Still, I admired him for showing spirit as he clenched his fists in a kind of a boxing move.

'No, not at all', I replied. I didn't want Simon's blood all over my good beige carpet. Anyway, the Slovenian was fixing me with his smoky eyes. 'Marko was a friend of Eithne's'.

Well, to cut to the chase, I never did manage to get away. For one thing, there's Zeus to stay home and mind. And then there's my new husband and the baby due in a couple of months. So much in my life has changed since those fateful days last year, they now seem like a dream. Each morning I wake squashed up against the wall by Marko, who fills most of the bed space. I still take Zeus down to join the Eleven O'Clockers, though my dependence on them has lessened considerably. Nevertheless, the walk does me good, as Marko tells me. He is very caring of me. We know the baby is a boy, which pleases him immensely.

Turns out the robbery was committed by some of Geeks' shadowy friends after he told them I had stuff worth fencing, as I believe the word is. One of them even tried to pawn the Patrick Swayze picture, not noticing the personal dedication which enabled it to be traced straight back to me. After the guards had been alerted they found the rest of the haul stashed in Deco Hanlon's garage.

Marko assures me, big hairy hand on heart, he had nothing to do with Geeks' death and I haven't pursued the matter. Do I really want to know what happened on the Ha'penny bridge in the dawn of a spring morning? No, the past is another country, as the man said, and we continue with our lives.

Marko is a treasure, really, and has not only redecorated and rewired the whole house but has even restored the kitchen floor to its pre-pee-stained glory (Zeus is firmly banished to an outside kennel). Nonetheless, I have taken the precaution, unbeknownst to my dear husband, of insuring his life for a nice round sum. It makes perfect sense, doesn't it, with a little one on the way. After all, when all's said and done, who can ever predict what fate, the bitch, has in store for any of us?

SUPERMAN

Barry was watching his wife as so often these days, as from a distance, as someone he hardly knew. There was grey in her hair, a furrow between her brows, tension had scored lines on her face. She was getting old.

He sighed. So was he. He was carrying too much weight, couldn't fly around the tennis court like he used to. Had to take up the more sedate game of golf. Which reminded him: he'd have to phone Andrew one way or the other.

He looked again at Joanna. So intent on what she was doing, the world, with him in it, excluded.

But could he leave her, the way she was, even for the weekend of the tournament? He didn't know. These days, he never seemed to know.

Joanna was building up the clay round the wire frame. She found the feel of the cold wet earth soothing, consoling even. Which was strange. You'd think it would set her off again: dust to dust, as the priest had said. But it was as if it kept her grounded, closer to Polly in some way.

'My best girl', she whispered, and smiled just a little.

It was another twisted body. Barry knew it would be. The room, Polly's room, was filled with them, a holocaust of corpses. The doctor said maybe it was a good thing, Joanna's way of coping, channelling her grief. Barry didn't know. It seemed weird to him. Now he had to clamber over clay bodies even to touch his wife.

'Joanna', he said.

He had to say it twice. Then she shook her head ever so slightly and turned distant eyes up to him.

'I was wondering, should I cancel it? ... The golf trip', he added when he saw she didn't know what he was talking about.

'No ... no. Go ahead'.

'But will you be all right?'

Then she smiled warmly, the old Joanna.

'Of course', she said. 'It'll do you good to get away'.

He felt guilty. He knew he would feel guilty again laughing with his friends in the pub. He would feel guilty in the exuberance of a summer's day swinging a long shot over the course fringed by Kerry hills. But only in passing. He would think of her with a twinge of remorse, and then forget, as he was almost frighteningly able to do. Was that how men coped, he wondered? Putting unpleasantness out of their heads. And then he smiled to himself: 'putting' was a pun. On the putting green.

Joanna couldn't wait to have him gone. It seemed he was constantly there, peering at her through his thick glasses, an uncomprehending expression on his face. Polly was his daughter too, of course. And yet after all these months the skin had grown back over his scars. Which was good. Which was how it should be. Only she couldn't let it. She tore at her scabs until they ran bloody again. Every day. Every minute. Her life measured in befores and afters.

A nice middle-class couple, like everyone else in the neighbourhood, in their three-bedroomed semi-detached with its bay windows and neat garden. Comfortably off although, like everyone they knew, they always complained that they didn't have enough. Especially after she gave up her job to look after the child. They'd discussed it. She'd said she wanted to, even if only for a year or two. He'd said they could manage. They wouldn't be going on those Mediterranean holidays for the foreseeable future. Or saving. Or going out to restaurants. And anyway childcare would have made a big hole in any money she might have earned. So she stayed home and minded the baby whose beauty made her gasp with wonder as she discovered extraordinary maternal depths within herself. Against her mother's advice – 'not once she gets teeth, Joanna, surely!' – she had breastfed for a year, becoming intoxicated with joy each time at the sensation of the hard little gums, the little teeth nuzzling hungrily.

Joanna coughed and slapped more damp clay on the twisted wire. What was she aiming for here? None of the figures were quite right. There was a space between some dark vision in her head and the shape before her, the broken child.

Yet Polly had died quiet and still in her bed. Not gasping for air, not bleeding, not broken. Just forgetting to breathe. That was one theory. The child forgets to breathe and dies in its cot. Two and a half years old. Not an uncommon phenomenon, it seemed.

'Do you smoke?' the insensitive nurse had asked.

'No'.

'Now that's unusual. Most cot deaths are to mothers who smoke'.

They'd checked them out, of course, performed an autopsy to rule out foul play. As if, as if. Yet everything was done, if done at all, discreetly. Their own doctor had, no doubt, had a word. Said what a nice comfortable middle-class couple they were. How they had doted, run to him at the slightest sniffle or rash.

'Polly's with the angels now', everyone told her until she wanted to scream out, 'fuck the angels!'

Barry phoned to ask how she was getting on.

'Fine, fine'.

'That's good'.

A pause.

'You're sure'.

'Yes, of course. Are you having a good time?'

'Great', he said before wondering if it was all right to admit to enjoying himself.

'That's good'.

'It's beautiful here'.

'Good'.

'What's it like there?'

She gazed out of the window at the clear blue sky.

'Nice'.

'You should get out. Go for a walk'.

'That's an idea'.

She hadn't intended to but the sun fell like a shower of gold through the window of Polly's room, across the clay dust, the heart-breaking little statues. And suddenly she'd had enough. Enough of this yellow room with its Winnie-the-Pooh wallpaper all that remained of the child's clutter.

'God willing, there'll be others', the nurse had said briskly, as if you swept one out to make room for the next.

Sometimes Joanna felt her continuing grief was irrational. Perhaps she should, as they all urged her, 'pull herself together' as if she was falling apart like her early figurines where the too-dry clay had crumbled away. She just couldn't do it. She knew they were right when they told her, in some exasperation, that she wasn't the first mother, nor would she be the last, to lose a child. The knowledge made it no easier. She felt joined to all the other bereft mothers who had howled over the centuries for their lost children. As she had, finding the cold small body. Rushing out into the garden to fall on the wet grass screaming as the skies wept with her and Barry had whispered to her to stop, to be quiet, she'd disturb the neighbours. How she'd hated him for that, for stepping back from grief, for already accepting the loss. How she had looked up at their nice little house with its pretty rooms and neat garden that now she saw were just a sham, just for show, where even the emotions had to be kept in order, acceptable to the neighbours. Like all those mothers over the centuries she'd howled and beaten the wet earth and cursed God and cursed Barry. And Dr O'Loughlin had given Barry pills to calm her, which she'd flushed down the lavatory.

Yes, she would get out of the house. Get out of the web of suburban streets that clutched with sticky strands. She drove on auto-pilot as if it was the car and not her that saw and avoided the parked van, the slick young man driving fast out of a side-street, the old woman on crutches. But when a mother pushed a buggy out into the road without looking, Joanna sat on her horn and shouted curses through the window, pins and needles shooting into her fingers.

She stopped at the park by the sea. Here they had brought Polly, fearing that she would teeter on her little fat legs over the edge of the path, tumbling down through ferns, because she would never hold hands, wanting to run off. And here Joanna's own mam and dad had brought Joanna when she herself was small, clutched tight, telling her not to climb trees in her nice dress, not to splash in the puddles. Which was why Joanna always let Polly have her way, let her come home like a mud monster. It would wash off.

And here Joanna had come with her friends, Marie and Tom and Vivienne and Donie, careering round on bikes down the steep slopes at top speed, falling sometimes, grazing elbows and knees. And later alone with Donie, her first love, crazy brave Donie, first and only one to the top of the tree, fastest down the steepest slope, with a freckled nose and mad hair, twelve years old among the shadows of the leafy trees, closed lips pressed chastely together before they ran off laughing under the stone bridge to the Folly.

The Folly. She had never gone that way since. Not told Barry why. In any case he always followed her path, never proposed another. Round by the stream where they tossed in leaves or berries to see whose would go fastest, past the monkey tree with its low branches that even Polly could climb on, Barry lifting her up and up until she was Queen of the Castle. Round to the wooden playground, where Polly never seemed to get tired of the swings, the wobbly wooden bridge. Never to the Folly.

But today she went deeper into the woods. No one was about: only in the far distance she could hear the excited calls of children. Bluebells the colour of Polly's eyes grew among pungent white-flowered ramsons, the way it had that far-off day. If only she could magically wipe away time and be there again, a girl, changing fate.

The young woman sitting at the bar smiled at Barry as he went up to buy his round. She was pert, with sharp-features.

'My friend likes you', she said, showing pointy little teeth.

Barry smiled back and over her shoulder at the plumper girl who turned red and punched her friend on the arm.

'Lilian!' she said. 'I'm scarlet'.

Barry didn't quite know what to say. He was pleased, of course, but these were county girls, thirtyish, desperate with waiting. White bellies loomed between tight tops and jeans. He returned to his mates, who roared with laughter when he told them.

'Don't lead him astray', Andrew called across to the women. 'He's a respectable married man'.

They giggled back.

Joanna stared. The Folly. A tower on a hill. The surrounding trees were higher now, brushing the top of the edifice with nervy branches. There would no longer be a view over them to the sea. And now even though the door was blocked off, graffiti was scrawled over the bricks, even high up. Kids always find a way.

Inside they had kissed, mouths closed because they didn't know any other way, among the bottles and remains of a bonfire. He had cupped her sprouting breast outside her t-shirt and then giggled because he really didn't know what to do next. Instead he had dashed away from her, past the warning sign, up the stone steps to the top of the tower.

'Donie!' she'd called, concerned.

'Wow, look at the view', he'd shouted. 'I can see the sea. Come on'.

But she was afraid. The steps curled up without a banister, the top was surmounted by only a low wall. Just to look made her feel dizzy. She ran outside.

'Come down, Donie. You eejit you'.

But he was running around the top of the folly with his arms stretched behind him as if he was flying, his mad hair flopping from side to side.

'Come down'. The panic in her voice made him laugh and laugh with glee and he ran even faster.

'I'm Superman!' he shouted.

She remembered now how Donie's mother had howled. At the time, weeping herself, but discreetly, she had thought it was like some animal sound. Joanna sat heavily on the ground, her back against the sharp bricks of the Folly. Everything changes in a moment, she thought. And then there's only befores and afters.

Barry and his friend went back to the pub after their game of golf. They were thirsty and hungry and lashed into the roast beef dinner. All of them were red-faced where they had caught the sun of the summer's day, already drunk with the heat.

The women were there, too, and kept glancing over and giggling. Somehow they looked prettier in the soft light.

It was like the old days, Barry thought. Before ...

Her mouth was soft and sticky. He couldn't remember her name – not Lilian, the other one – but it didn't seem to matter. They were in the dark against the back wall outside the pub and his hands grabbed at the roll of bare flesh between her top and her jeans. He tried to push his hand down inside, but her belt was too tight, her belly too big.

She laughed and aimed his hand up under her top, to her armoured breasts. He fumbled there while she undid his trousers. A door opened, a light came on.

'Christ!' he exclaimed.

'Shh', she giggled.

The door shut, the light went out.

Joanna told them he had fallen. That he was running so fast he had lost his balance. And who would have doubted her? They all knew what he was like. Mad as a hatter. An accident waiting to happen.

They didn't question her for long. She was hysterical. They didn't want her to come to the funeral but she insisted. All energy gone, she just wept quietly. Unlike Donie's mam.

But now among the bluebells and pungent ramsons as the sun showered gold through the leaves, puddling on the earth, she remembered how he had dashed away from her, up the steps, how he had called to her.

'No, you come down', she had cried in a panic. 'You'll fall'.

'I won't fall. I'm Superman'.

He had jumped. Mad Donie had tried to fly off the top of the Folly, showing off, laughing as he leapt.

How his mother had howled as they tipped his box into the clay.

'Dust to dust', intoned the priest.

'No!' she screamed.

Everyone looked at each other. Later, his mother was dead quiet, with distant eyes. Joanna's mam said they'd had to give her pills.

It was after the accident they blocked off the door. Everyone blamed the council for not blocking it off earlier. It could have happened to any one of our children, they said to each other.

People were sorry for Joanna, that she'd been witness to such a horror and her mother held her tight.

Barry, eaten with guilt – but mildly, blame the drink, the sunshine – couldn't understand why Joanna didn't answer the phone. He had been trying on and off for hours. If she'd asked him he would have gone home early, not stayed for the final night. It would be her fault if anything happened. Anything else. He rejoined his mates.

The entry was blocked off, but the wood, after so many years, was rotten. Joanna pulled at it. A little came away. She needed a lever. Among the fallen leaves she found a branch strong but not too thick and, after considerable effort, prised the door away sufficiently so that she could slip through the gap.

A stunted bush grew inside the tower. The stone steps curled up, covered with lichen. Still full of dread, still vertiginous, she started to climb up, close against the wall. She kept looking at the steps, not up, not down, until she reached the top. Sitting heavily on the stone floor, gasping for breath, panicky. Hearing the wind slough through the leaves of the surrounding high trees as they reached out towards the top of the tower.

Then she saw it. Carved into the parapet – J+D surrounded with a heart – carved with Donie's penknife.

And suddenly she remembered. After all the years. Crawling up the steps while he'd laughed down at her, grasping his hand as he pulled her up, panicky and gasping.

How he'd laughed and then said kindly, 'it's not so high, is it. Not really'.

And then she'd laughed and they kissed, lips hard on lips. And he'd taken out his penknife and carved their initials and she'd taken the knife and drawn the heart around them.

Then he'd held her while she stood on the parapet and looked out over the treetops to the sea.

She had come up here. She had come up here to join him. Now she remembered. And it was she who had said it.

'If you're superman', she'd said. 'Then you can fly'.

And he'd stretched out his hand to her like Superman to Lois Lane and she'd taken it and they'd stood together on the parapet. Because they were in love and everything was possible.

But at the last moment he'd dropped her hand or she his and he'd leapt off alone.

And for a moment, Joanna had believed that indeed he would spread his wings and take off over the treetops, flying off to save the world.

That was why her Polly had been taken from her. A life for a life.

Now, remembering, she knew why she'd got it all so wrong. She'd been looking at it all from the wrong angle. Now she knew how the statue should look, one leg curled back under, the head loose on the neck, the arms apart, like broken wings.

She knew how the statue should look. Now she could make the statue right.

So she jumped.

GRAND GUIGNOL

The old man placed a quivering hand on the manuscript. Twisted twigs of fingers. Fist spotted as a toad's back.

'I can't let you have this', he whispered. His voice was the wind in dry grasses.

'Why not?'

'Too dangerous'.

'Come now. That's ridiculous'. The singer eyed the manuscript hungrily. 'Can't I even look at it?'

The old man sighed. His fingers trembled more. 'Not a good idea', he said. 'Believe me'.

The singer sighed too. He was more certain than ever that what he had been looking for lay on the table under the old man's feeble hand. He didn't know why he was so sure. Maybe, after all the searching through clean, airy music stores, where white sheets lay in regimented piles, the songs he had never sung, never wanted to sing, as bland and banal as the setting, it seemed that here, in this dusty dump of a shop, hitherto undiscovered treasures had to be buried. The place smelt of decay, filled as it was with damp heaps of books and manuscripts. It was windowless, the only light a class of an oil lamp. The singer glanced up at the ceiling, once long ago painted the bluey-black of the night sky, but now with whitish patches of mould creeping across it, like some ghastly premonition of dawn. What was the old man playing at? Looked like he could do with the money. Maybe he was holding out for a higher offer. The singer named a price. Absurd of course when he hadn't even seen the thing. Hadn't even heard of the composer. But he was so sure.

The old man shook his head. 'No, no'.

Of course, the singer could have snatched the manuscript off the table, flinging down some coins and escaping with his prize. He was young and strong and could easily have overpowered an old man. But that wasn't his style.

'Why dangerous?' he asked. 'How could it be?'

The old man muttered something. A crackle in the throat.

'What?'

Louder now. 'A curse. There's a curse on it'.

The singer threw back his head and laughed. In this day and age!

'It's true. Men have died singing this'.

'I'll take that risk'.

'You don't know what you're saying. The composer ...' The old man stopped.

'Yes?'

'The composer sold his soul to write this'.

'Did he indeed? What, to the devil?'

'Not to God, anyway'. The old man's face stretched into the semblance of a grin, a death's head in the flickering gloom.

But the singer took it as a good sign. A shifting, a softening. 'You see', he said, 'I've been looking a long time for a new piece. I've exhausted the repertoire and in any case ...' Should he confess his motive? Why not? What had he to lose? 'Others have made all those song cycles their own. The definitive *Winterreise* has already been sung. *Dichterliebe. An die ferne Geliebte.* Wolf's songbooks, both Italian and Spanish ... I can't compete with my predecessors on those. I want something new. Something that can be exclusively mine'.

The old man stared at the singer for a long time, eyes flaming like sudden sparks in a fire you thought was dying. 'Ah, the vanity of youth', he said at last. 'I had forgotten that'.

The singer felt the other consuming him with those eyes. He shivered.

'Let me hear you sing', the old man said at last. 'To find out if you are worthy'.

'Sing? Here?'

'You're a singer, aren't you? What could be more natural for you?'

'What do you want to hear?'

'Ah ... It's my choice, is it?' Again the old man grinned. The singer shivered again. Was there a draught? The door was shut. There were no windows.

'The last song of *Winterreise,* then. It's a particular favourite of mine'.

'*Der Leiermann*?'

'Yes'.

'Without accompaniment?'

'I can accompany you'.

Still holding the precious manuscript, the old man shuffled off his chair and over to an upright piano, looming out of deep shadow, covered in broken books.

'Bring the lamp', the old man said.

The singer picked it up, a thing of tarnished brass, surely an antique. It cast wildly dancing shadows as he made his way across the shop, dodging the obstacles in his path. If he rubbed it with his sleeve, what genii would appear? What spirit to make wishes come true? He balanced the lamp on the books on top of the piano and the shadows steadied.

'Well then', the old man said.

'I don't know'.

'You don't know the song?'

'Of course I do. But to sing it here ... Cold'.

'You're cold?'

'Yes, actually'. The singer felt frozen. How had that happened? 'But that's not what I mean'.

'I don't expect a definitive performance'. The old man cackled, laughter rattling in his throat. 'But you see, young man', he went on, 'it's your only chance of getting hold of this'. Shaking the manuscript under the singer's nose.

'I'll try'.

The old man hunched over the piano and from memory started to play those first sinister little notes. The piano's tone was an ancient jangle, just like a hurdy-gurdy, and the singer's voice shook as he closed his eyes and started to sing. But as he launched himself deeper into the piece, it was as if he were swept out of the dusty shop and into icy cold wastes following the barefoot old organ-grinder. His voice grew truer as he became that lonely wanderer. All his pent-up longing expressed in the final cry: *'Shall I join you on your journey? Will you play the music to my songs?'*

It was finished. The singer opened his eyes.

The old man picked up the manuscript and held it out to him.

'Take it, then', he said. 'But remember I have warned you'.

The singer snatched at the sheets.

'Be careful', the old man said. 'It's fragile. It could fall apart at any moment'.

Indeed, the paper was so light the singer was hardly aware of holding anything at all. In the dim glow from the oil lamp, he had to squint to make out the faint code of notes. Then, in his growing excitement, he forgot everything else. Turning the pages, greedily eating in the songs. 'This is it', he sighed finally. 'This is what I've been looking for. Much more than I hoped. Oh my God!' He looked at the old man, but the other's face was in darkness. 'How much do you want for this? Anything you ask. Anything'.

'Nothing', the old man replied sadly. 'My reward, my punishment will be hearing you sing it'.

The young man forgot the curse, or if he remembered it in the following months, it was with a shake of the head and a smile. The old man had said men had died. Who, then? The singer had omitted to ask. But wouldn't he have heard about it before? Such a story would have entered the mythology, no doubt about it, like the superstition connected to the writing of a ninth symphony. He asked his friend Jacob, a musician, but Jacob hadn't heard of any such curse either.

'Who is this composer anyway?' he asked.

'It's a scribble on the manuscript. Looks like Abraham or Alhambra or something similar. I've looked up all possible variant spellings but nothing's come up'.

'Perhaps it's a pseudonym'.

'What do you mean?'

'The piece is so accomplished, the composer must surely have written other things. Maybe for some reason in this case he wanted to conceal his identity'.

The singer considered this.

'For instance', Jacob went on, 'maybe he made his name writing trashy popular songs and didn't want people to associate this piece with that sort of garbage'.

'Seems unlikely'.

'Not at all. I do it myself'.

The singer looked in surprise at the merry face of his friend.

'Only the other way round. I use my own name for my serious pieces and a pseudonym for things I don't want my friends and fans to know about'.

'Like what?'

'Like jingles for ads. Bread-and-butter stuff. You know'.

The singer, who had on past occasions been hungry enough to resort to such work, nodded.

The two friends worked together in deep secrecy on the cycle of seven songs and Jacob soon became as enthusiastic as the singer was. The date of the concert was set. Posters went up over town showing the singer looking suitably saturnine, that toss of dark fringe over glowering eyes smudged purple, the sharply prominent cheekbones in a chalk-white face, his lean body swathed in a black cloak. Articles were written in prestigious newspapers and magazines speculating on the substance of the concert, the nature and origins of the hitherto unknown composition. The singer, up to now regarded as a promising but not spectacular performer, was even invited on to a television chat show where he refused to give a taste or even a hint of the new work, choosing to regale the audience with a light-hearted Rossini aria instead.

Christmas came and went, deep in snow. The old year died and the new was heralded with the usual foolish expectation that things would be better, come the spring.

It was the last day of January and people trudged through slush to the concert hall. The advertising had worked, something had worked, and the performance was sold out. Despite the chill, a long snake of people curled around the hall. Steam rose from damp coats, from expelled breath, as the lucky ones shuffled into the foyer, where marble pillars rose yellow as dead stalks from the marble floor, and where dusty red velvet stools wobbled on chipped gilt legs around walls covered in torn paper flocked with blood-red flowers. The hall had seen better days, but now thrilled with expectant life, like some faded beauty, ever hopeful.

You rummage for your ticket and finally find it in your pocket, passing it to be inspected. The attendant rips off a narrow strip and hands you back the rest. It is the magic key entitling you to cross the threshold into the hall itself where a crooked old man in a shiny dress suit and black bow tie points you to your seat, more padded crimson, but everywhere stained or discoloured. You sit back and fold your coat over your lap, then raise your eyes to the garishly painted dome, illuminated by a huge and tarnished chandelier, depicting Euterpe, muse of music, playing on a flute, while Terpsichore, one plump pink breast bared, dances around her. Then you lower your eyes to the stage where a grand piano crouches like a giant beetle, its lid raised on one shiny black wing. You stand up to let people pass you to reach their seats: a fat woman whose silk-clad backside slides against your thighs, a plain young girl with spectacles and magnificent golden hair halfway down her back, a thin bald man, who says 'sorry, sorry, sorry'. You study the programme, the text of songs never before heard, obscure words that tremble in front of your eyes. At the last minute, as the lights go down and as a voice tells you to look for your nearest exit in the unlikely event of a fire, someone tumbles into the aisle seat beside you, a very old man, his skinny fingers digging at your arm as though to stop himself from falling into some bottomless pit.

Two men walk on to the stage to the accompaniment of polite applause. For who knows yet if they'll deserve it. They are beautiful as young men can often be. The smaller of the two, with a crown of ginger curls, seats himself at the piano and adjusts the pages of his score, then looks up expectantly at the other, lean and as haunted-looking as he is on the posters, the lock of dark hair that falls across his smudged eyes tossed away with long pale fingers, only to fall and fall again.

He stares at the floor for several long minutes and you feel yourself getting restless. The fat woman fidgets, a rustle of silk. The girl's eyes fix on the stage, inscrutable behind her thick glasses. The thin man coughs. The singer finally looks up and nods at the pianist who strikes the first chord. The first discord. You start to follow the written words but soon the programme falls from your lap as the songs entwine you. A rootless spirit wanders through bare mountains, hopeless and troubled. He is alone, his heart heavy. The second song finds him in a valley, unseen by the peasants working their land together. The spirit imagines their happy comradeship in contrast to his loneliness, and he cries out with anguish against his destiny. You shiver in response.

In the next song the spirit sees lovers embracing in a field of flowers. He yearns for love in a minor key, without hope, for he is condemned to be forever alone. The fourth song finds him at a wedding. People feast and he wants to share their meat and drink. But he is a spirit and cannot partake. Again he cries out but no one can hear him. He flees from the scene.

The fifth song finds him following a trill of music to a waterfall, where he comes upon a boy playing a flute. The sweet music causes silvery fish to leap from the splashing water to the feet of the boy who laughs with innocent delight. Suddenly, the spirit springs at the boy's throat and takes his laughter, leaving him dumb. You gasp. The whole audience gasps. You feel the old man next to you quiver and shudder.

The spirit next returns to the wedding feast, but the guests have left. A half moon illuminates the desolate scene. But wait! Who is this half in shadow? It is the husband embracing his new wife. Filled with uncontrollable desire, the spirit flings off his cloak of invisibility, striking the husband dead with a bolt from his burning eyes. He carries off the girl, laughing as he goes, while she trembles in terror. 'I will be alone no more!' he shouts in triumph and presses his lips to hers. The song pauses on a high note which turns into a scream and tumbles down three octaves. The girl has turned to ashes in his arms, cremated by his kiss.

The final song has the spirit wandering, hopeless and alone again. He sees the purple clouds behind mist-blue mountains, shot through with gold from the setting sun. But what is this beauty to him now?

As the singer hits the last note his voice cracks. He stumbles, he falls. The audience, about to celebrate with wild applause, holds its breath. All but your neighbour, who pulls himself to his feet and shuffles to the stage, where even now the pianist crouches over his friend.

The old man tenderly lifts the singer's head.

From where you sit, you can hear his words. His tremulous voice.

'I told you', he says, 'not to sing my songs. I told you there was a curse. You wouldn't listen. And now you will die and I will be forced to spend another lifetime here alone'.

He kisses the singer full on the mouth and as he does so you see the dying man give one last sighing breath. The pianist, still kneeling at his side, suddenly leaps to his feet with a scream and rushes from the stage. Rushes out of the concert hall. The old man looks up. But an old man no longer. He lets the singer's head fall, then stands up, tall and strong, with long black hair that flows over his shoulders like a cape. He locks his eyes on yours, on the eyes of every terrified person present. They burn with white heat.

'You will forget what you have seen', he says. 'Forget all that you have heard. I envy you that you can forget so easily'.

He looks down again at the singer.

'He is lucky too', he says. 'At least he can die'.

Then he leaps from the stage and flies out the door and as he does so a blast of air scatters the heap of ashes lying on the stage until there is nothing left of it. Nothing at all.

A storm blew up that night. Such a storm people had never seen before. Or only the very old, recalling another such night in the distant past. It uprooted strong trees and tore tiles from roofs so that they clashed to the ground in cacophonous percussion. It glutted the river with rain until it overflowed its banks, angry waves washing down the streets of the town and carrying away with it anything not anchored to the ground, children's toys abandoned in gardens, garbage bins, even cars. The wind and rain whipped at outer walls and ripped the posters of the singer, clawing at them until they hung in unrecognisable shreds, to be torn off by violent gusts and swallowed up into the maw of darkness. No one ventured out but huddled with others behind barricaded doors, trying to close their ears against the shrieks of the tempest. No one was out.

But yes, there was one, a madman with ginger curls, flung along the streets of the town by the buffeting blasts, his arms flailing in the air as if to stop himself from drowning. Then suddenly tossed on a whirl of wind up into a birch tree where he stayed clinging to the thickest branch until the gale died down and the ghastly light of dawn crept in, a chalky whiteness scribbling strange scripts across the blue-black page of night. There they found him the next day, singing in a cracked voice, a musician, someone said, but as for the music he was singing, nothing melodious there at all. And never would be again.

ACKNOWLEDGEMENTS

Grateful thanks to everyone who provided support, positive criticism and insights into areas where I lacked expertise, especially Phyl Herbert, Ken Ward and Leo Crowley. To Niamh Boyce for her kind words. To Maev Lenaghan for her lovely cover illustrations. And above all to Alan Hayes and his amazing Arlen House for trusting me enough to publish this collection.

About the Author

Susan Knight is the author of three novels, *The Invisible Woman* (Poolbeg, 1993), *Grimaldi's Garden* (Marino, 1995) and *Gomorrah* (Fairground Press, 2007), as well as a previous collection of stories, *Letting Rip* (Original Writing, 2012). In addition she compiled and edited a non-fiction book, *Where the Grass is Greener: Voices of Immigrant Women in Ireland* (Oak Tree Press, 2001), two sections of which were included in the *Field Day Anthology of Irish Literature: Irish Women's Writing and Traditions,* Vol. V (2001). She has written a number of plays, most recently *A Simple Twist of Fate,* performed at the Viking Theatre in Dublin in 2014, and has received several prizes for her short stories and stage and radio plays, including the James Plunkett Memorial Award, the Bryan McMahon Award, the Molly Keane Award, and the premier award in the P.J. O'Connor radio play competition. She teaches creative writing and gives lectures on literature for the Shaw Trust. She lives in Dublin.